More Money for Good

Franklin White

URBAN
RENAISSANCE

www.urbanbooks.net

Urban Books, LLC
97 N18th Street
Wyandanch, NY 11798

More Money for Good Copyright © 2013 Franklin White

ISBN 13: 978-1-60162-392-8
ISBN 10: 1-60162-392-5

First Trade Paperback Printing September 2013
Printed in the United States of America

10 9 8 7 6 5 4 3 2 1

This is a work of fiction. Any references or similarities to actual events, real people, living or dead, or to real locales are intended to give the novel a sense of reality. Any similarity in other names, characters, places, and incidents is entirely coincidental.

Distributed by Kensington Publishing Corp.
Submit Wholesale Orders to:
Kensington Publishing Corp.
C/O Penguin Group (USA) Inc.
Attention: Order Processing
405 Murray Hill Parkway
East Rutherford, NJ 07073-2316
Phone: 1-800-526-0275
Fax: 1-800-227-9604

The Night Before

For good reason Tavious Bell is mentally exhausted. Exactly twenty years have passed and now in a matter of hours he will be free. For the past year, simply sitting in a holding cell waiting for release from Jesup Federal Correctional Institute just outside Savannah, Georgia, has only been a dream, but now reality.

Inside the cell there is a shower, single toilet, a window looking out to nowhere, and private access to a phone free for calling. Tavious sits still, close to shock, as his new clothes sent from his grandmother from Atlanta are on his bunk staring back at him. He hasn't decided to change just yet because his emotions are all over the place, because 7,300 days of being behind bars under someone's control is a hell of a calculation to endure for any man—even if he has two million waiting for him on the outside.

It's difficult for Tavious to control his emotions. He is a nervous wreck and promised himself for weeks that he wouldn't let this moment be this way. Freakin' sitting down and thinking about leaving this place for the last time in his mind is definitely worse than having ten years left on the books. He continuously struggles to gather his composure and relax, seeing that being on the outside is no longer the same as two decades ago. So, just like so many times before during his 175,200 hours inside, he decides to make a call to help him get through his troublesome anxieties of becoming an unbound man of the State of Georgia.

"Hey," he says softly. Whispering into the phone is going to be one of many inside habits he's going to have to break.

"Hey, you!" the lady's voice squeals with anticipation on the other end. "Are you out already?"

He exhales at the thought. "No, no . . . I'm in holding 'til morning."

"Man, you know it wouldn't have been a problem to drive down and pick you up," her sweet voice echoes. "I would have drove and sat outside in my car all night, for you."

"Really?"

"Really."

He smiles at the thought. "No, that would have been too much. Plus, I'm going to need the time to focus— get my equilibrium of being out together."

"And how are you going to do that? Tavious, it's a process, right?"

"Yeah, I gotta walk around some, hear, smell, and see how it is out there before I see you."

"I understand," she tells him.

"I mean, I don't want to spook you out when you first lay eyes on me."

She sighs in anticipation. "Just don't take forever to get here, okay? I miss you. . . ."

"I miss you too." Tavious notices a faint giggle on the other end. "What's so funny?"

"I just realized this is the first time in twenty years you haven't called me collect . . . that's all."

Tavious glances around his cell. Even though he is still locked up, the cell is much better than the place he has been calling home. The State of Georgia Corrections hadn't quite gotten it right. There could have been a few more amenities; more fresh towels, a better color TV with cable to watch— that news station stays on all hours of the night—and upgraded sheets to help him with his transition to the outside, he thinks, but his new digs will definitely do, at least for the night.

"Yeah, it's crazy," he lets her know. "Before I called, I sat with the phone on my ear for at least twenty minutes waiting for the operator before I realized I could just dial out. I guess there's going to be a lot of things I will have to get used to," he confirms.

"Don't worry, I'll walk you through."

"Promise?"

"Yeah, I promise."

There is silence on the phone now. The never-wavering connection of the two who have been linked together unconditionally as friends for the entire 630,720,000 seconds of reform are realizing they have conquered and endured the imposed time placed on Tavious Bell by the State of Georgia.

After a few minutes she calls out, "Tavious?"

"Yeah?"

"Remember when I told you I wouldn't cry twenty years ago when they walked you out of the courtroom?" she reflects. "Well, I didn't. Nor did I during or after any of our thousands of phone calls we've had. Not even on my one and only visit when you were halfway through this. I swear to you, I haven't the entire time and it's been hard not to."

"And I appreciate it," Tavious lets her know. "You've been so strong and I needed that."

She starts talking before Tavious finishes. "But this time, I can't hold it," she barely lets out and tears are already rolling down her face. "You're finally coming home."

There's absolutely no way Tavious can ask his friend to hold her emotions in. It has happened before because hearing her cry would make him lose the focus it required for him to do his time. But now his time is done and it takes everything inside of him not to join her as she begins to shed tears and he finally lets her have her day.

Part 1

Chapter 1

The last words Tavious Bell ever heard as a free man over twenty years ago came from the mouths of hard-boiled DEA agents screaming for him to freeze or they'd blow his freakin' head off. In 1991 that was how it was done because back then nobody cared; at least, they didn't act like they did, and, to make matters worse, cameras and phones didn't saturate the streets to record the daily brutality being handed out to headstrong, money-hungry, fatherless seventeen-year-old dope-pushing black boys.

Now thirty-eight-year-old Tavious Bell was two hours fresh out of prison and stood in the exact spot where his freedom had been taken. He thought by going back to a familiar corner it would help him to get acclimated to the outside again. But consequently things were not going as planned, especially after the terrifying cab ride from prison with a cab driver who seemed to be going over a hundred miles an hour, swearing all the way he wasn't going a tick over thirty-five.

Once the car finally stopped its high-speed, Indy-500 jaunt, Tavious finally had his feet back on the ground. He buckled over and spewed out decades of repulsive prison food that had been encrusted into his system. This had lasted at least thirty minutes.

Bell promised he wouldn't let it happen but already being locked up twenty years had taken its toll. His entire symmetry was off in the streets that he would once roam at all hours of the night. Anyone could understand his confusion with his release into a world twenty years older. He had questions, just like those living on the outside who had been screaming at their politicians on a daily basis. *Why were there so many homeless people? The streets and atmosphere had become darker, harder, ugly, in fact.* The busy streets he once knew—with pretty young things walking and talking, strutting their stuff along with traffic—were bare. There were so many brothers standing around the same way they did back at the yard with the same exact lifeless expressions. He knew those faces all too well. Not faces of happy men. On the inside if guards noticed the same sort of solemn look of despair and tension, the entire prison would be locked down for at least two weeks to prevent a riot or rebellion. This reunion was nothing like the happening days when Tavious supplied the whole damn city with Mary Jane to smoke.

Damn. What happened to the city?

Tavious realized that he needed to battle through his memories of the streets and deal with the reality at hand. Fight through the fact that when the Feds got him with the dope . . . It was one hell of a celebrated case. Perp walk for the cameras. News conference with the drugs sprawled out on the table. Finally, they celebrated and cheered that their long hours of surveillance had paid off. They got everything they thought. Everything but the money.

That was why the twenty years in the pen was doable. His stashed money on the outside waiting for him kept him going in prison all the way to the point where he had the next twenty years of his life on a blueprint. And, now, he was free, without any of the worries most just-released ex-cons had to deal with. His main concern was fighting desperately to get his bearings and get back to a life as he never had known as a rich man.

The first order of business was to make a phone call. Tavious wanted to call Amara to let her know he was okay. While in prison he never could imagine as stories and tales from the streets filtered in with every new batch of convicts brought in. But it was true: all the phones on corners, the ones he called his connects for re-up supplies, were no more. He needed a TracFone: the same kind that were smuggled inside the prison.

With a portion of the $500 balance he was given from his account in prison, Tavious purchased a twenty-dollar phone with a hundred minutes of usage. A downtown corner sandwich shop played host for setting up his charge while he ordered up and down the menu of the undeniable specialty sandwiches for his depleted stomach. In the time that it took his phone to charge a few bars, and to the amazement of his waitress, he ordered three sandwiches. A double hamburger with fries, corn beef with fries, and an Italian sub with fries. Before he devoured each sandwich he studied them like pieces of art before enjoying their essence of smell and taste. *Finally.*

With his phone now charged enough to make his calls Tavious opened his black address book. It was the only item he kept from the inside. He scanned the numbers, closed it, and began to call Amara, not because he forgot the number but because *he could* and there was no one who could tell him that *he couldn't.* Amara's digits he would never forget. Everyone who knew Tavious when he ran the streets was aware that Amara had been his right hand back in the day when they were young bucks making a name for themselves. They had traveled to and from Miami together when he was busted. She had been the reason no money was found with the drugs the Feds confiscated. They didn't ride the same bus on the way back and all the money was in her possession when he was hoisted off to prison. All on the word of a snitch who offered the info to the Feds because he wanted more product and Tavious didn't think he was ready.

It was odd for Tavious using the phone as a free man. From habit he looked around a few times to see if anyone was trying to listen to what he was about to say. He looked at the phone and kind of chuckled. He was free. He dialed and placed it on his ear. He wanted to pull a cord. Subconsciously he waited for the operator to appear again to connect his call. There were no recording beeps like in prison. Immediately during the first ring the phone was picked up.

"Hello?" Amara was on the receiving end. She can't even hide she'd been sitting by the phone waiting his call since they spoke the night before.

Tavious cleared his voice. "Amara? It's Tavious."

She shrieked. "It better be you . . . I can't believe this," she said.

"Believe it, baby. I'm back," Tavious said, looking around the diner, getting energy from his freedom and stuffing another fry into his mouth just because he could again.

"So where are you?" Amara needed to know.

"Downtown."

She could hear him smacking on his fries and she pushed like she really wanted to. "You want me to come for you?"

Tavious smiled at her eagerness. "No, no. I'm on my way over about an hour or so. I just needed to take a little more in. It's different out here, Amara—so fast."

"Baby steps, Tavious," she encouraged.

"I'm good," he let her know. "Hey, I see those pad things you were telling me about."

"An iPad." She giggled.

"Yeah, those. Seems like everybody up in here has one. I'm going to get one."

Tavious looked into the phone at the sound of Amara laughing, getting close to hysterically. She finally stopped. "Hold on, man, we can do all that later. You need to get your butt over here. Let's just sit down, talk, count this—"

Tavious interrupted. "No, Amara. Not on the phone . . . even though I'm out, never on the phone. We can catch up when I get there okay?"

"Well, I've made the reservations for our vacation. I'm just waiting on you to get here."

"How'd you do that so fast? We just spoke about getting away."

"The computer, Tavious . . . it's so easy to do."

Tavious was close to hitting the wall. It was becoming overwhelming. Poor people on the streets in overwhelming numbers and technology that made it seem like he was now on another planet.

"You okay, Tavious? Tavious?" Amara repeated.

"Oh yeah, I'm fine. I'll see you soon."

Chapter 2

A little over an hour later Tavious thanked his cabby for rolling at a smooth, steady speed to his destination. He smashed twenty dollars into the cab driver's hand, stepped out of the ride, and made his way up the driveway toward Amara's residence. He scanned her place.

Good; not too flashy. She hasn't been spending any of the money, just like she promised.

She lived on Beecher Street in southwest Atlanta. For Tavious, it barely looked like the same house as twenty years ago, the same neighborhood even. His mind wanders back to the time when he was younger. He can't place what his eyes were seeing; back in the day he didn't pay much attention to the aesthetics of his surroundings because he was always on the move, never stopping to smell the roses or enjoying anything longer than a moment. But he is sure what he was seeing had drastically changed and he didn't want to focus on that fact because it was like a downer. He'd already had enough of those.

A rust-colored Camry that appeared to be well taken care of sat parked close to the walkway to the door with the front end pointing toward the street. He smiled, remembering they always used to park that way in case they needed a quick getaway.

Tavious looked over his shoulders a few times before he reached the door, then once again before he knocked. Close to fifteen seconds elapsed before he tapped on it again and then he waited another fifteen to knock so as not to appear too anxious. Still waiting at the door after knocking, then ringing the bell, he looked around at the homes on each side next door to make sure he was at the right house. There was absolutely no movement inside. Tavious smashed his face on the windowed doorframe to look inside, even opened his little black book to make sure he was at the right address. He could barely see inside the curtained window on the frame of the door. He called out for Amara before knocking again. He pulled out his phone and called her. He could hear the phone ringing from inside. Tavious put his phone in his pocket, then put his hand on the doorknob, then pushed, and it opened.

He stood still for a moment, looking around and calling out for Amara. She doesn't answer and he stepped into the small foyer of the house, shutting the door behind him. With widened eyes, Tavious scanned the inside while he wondered where Amara was. Memories of being in the three-bedroom house were becoming surreal. With a smile he called out for her, remembering all too well how she liked to surprise him back in the day. *This is probably one of those times.*

After searching the downstairs of the house, through the kitchen, and taking a look-see into the family room and even the garage, Tavious was hesitant about going upstairs. He didn't think long about going up but his survival skills of being inside kicked in. He felt like he had to make a vital decision of venturing to the unguarded stalls out on the yard to urinate or holding himself until back inside his cell. Despite his wavering he ventured upstairs cautiously, noticing the squeaky third and fourth steps. When he reached the top of the staircase he could see Amara wearing blue jeans, a fitted black T-shirt without any shoes, lying on her back completely still in a pool of blood that was inches from running down the steps.

Tavious can't get to her fast enough. After calling her name over and over he reached down to see if she was alive. She looked exactly the same as he remembered. He cried out her name this time and could feel his heart begin to beat faster at a panic pace. At the touch of his hand Amara's body doesn't move or react. Tavious never learned any medical procedures on the inside other than to see if someone was breathing, and he put his ear close to her mouth.

She was dead. Her body was still warm and eyes wide open as though she wanted to tell someone what had happened. Tavious only wished she could. But there was one word that blasted over and over in his head: *leave!*

He dare not stay any longer to try to figure out what happened; he couldn't, he was fresh out of prison. But he knew she had been murdered. There was no denying that. The pool of blood came from the hole in the back of her head. Tavious closed Amara's eyes and finally his own tears began to roll down his face. He hadn't planned to see her this way. Panic was soon to control his every move and he didn't like that feeling. In a hurry, he scanned the hallway while leaning over Amara's body to see if his money was anywhere around, but the hallway was clear.

Tavious can't take the shock and panic that was beginning to take over his body but still he knew that he needed to find his money. All the years inside Amara never told him where she hid it other than hinting in the house with her. His distress barely let him stand, his legs were heavy, but when he did, he ran through every room looking for the two million. After a few minutes he realized and reached the reality of the moment. Amara was dead and his money gone.

Chapter 3

That morning my watch read nine thirty-two. I was expecting Mrs. Shirley Bullock any minute for our meeting. Actually I'd been waiting since nine but there was no way I would ever put a time limit on the woman responsible for helping me get out of the catastrophe of a jam I'd found myself in during jury duty back in 2004. I was at my wit's end: no money, repairing cars on the street in front of where I lived, and on jury duty. Then I made the mistake and put my nose where it didn't belong in a case sent to the jury. The Atlanta Police Department and district attorney were hot on my ass. I had become connected with my now good friend, Pete Rossi—someone they wanted very much to put in jail—and of course there was the money.

My cup of coffee was exactly what I'd expected from my favorite diner on Moreland Avenue. The day I had planned required that I be full of caffeine to help me get through it. Payroll, check repair sheets, then more payroll. I'd brought along my books that Lauren had prepared for me for final review before I paid the guys at the shop. Right along with it were the receipts for the past two weeks. I was praying it would be enough to cover the payroll and send everyone home to feed their families.

There was no hiding that the economy was biting everyone hard, even my repair shop; it seemed as though people were driving their cars longer with problems they knew they had and not caring one damn bit that it would cost them more in the long run. Even worse was all the chatter customers would bombard me with into giving them a deal, discount, or the all-time-favorite "hookup" on repairs.

Mrs. Bullock had a driver now. She had finally taken my advice of getting someone to accompany her back and forth from the many business meetings and community forums she attended. Besides that, it wasn't safe in the streets anymore. The way these young bucks were jumping into cars and holding drivers at gunpoint had even made me go get my permit to carry. If someone thought they were going to ever jump in my ride and take my business income before I could deposit it in the bank, they were in for a hot surprise of lead.

Mrs. Bullock's driver opened the door for her as she strolled in the diner with each careful step, and saying hello to a few people who recognized her along the way. I stood up and walked down to receive her, and led her to our table. I assisted with her coat, then waited until she sat down before I took my seat. She was definitely still royalty in Atlanta. In my eyes she was in the sphere of Coretta Scott King, and all the other strong women who played a role in the Civil Rights era.

She smiled like she always does.

"I have a pot of hot water right here for you, Mrs. Bullock," I let her know.

"Oh, thank you, dear," she said back. Then she said, "I'm going to get you to hold some classes, West, for some of these youngsters on how to treat a lady." She smiled.

I just smiled back at her and enjoyed her comment. She turned over her cup. I began to slightly pour her water. As the steam appeared, she picked up her tea bag and opened it. When I was finished, she placed it inside the cup and it began to steep.

"So, how are you, West? I see you're going over paperwork for the shop no doubt?"

"I'm fine . . . just making sure the money keeps flowing and matches up with what's going out later today."

"Payday?"

"Absolutely, the reason we all work," I let her know. I will never forget she helped with all the startup money for making my dream of owning a shop a reality.

She said, "I've always said, you remind me of my late husband. Such a stickler for making sure . . . Checks and balances . . . checks and balances."

Mrs. Bullock making reference to her husband about me was cool. One of the most powerful men to ever walk the streets of Atlanta, and to be compared to him was an honor. It was her idea that we actually meet at the diner but I wasn't going to rush her as to the reason why. So, I waited until she was ready to talk to me.

Mrs. Bullock ordered a slice of toast with grape jam. I drank another cup of coffee while we visited.

"So, how's my grandson making out at the shop?" she wanted to know.

Mrs. Bullock was referring to Tavious. I'd hired him out of respect for her after his stretch in prison. He'd been working in the shop about two months. I assured her that he was doing a great job. His job training on the inside had not gone wasted. Matter of fact he was the only worker in the shop who wasn't busting my balls and giving me any back talk about the new lean workforce habits I wanted my shop workers to follow.

"Just thought I'd ask," Mrs. Bullock relayed. "To me . . . he seems a little on edge. Like a man who is greatly disappointed."

I was putting down my coffee cup, but she was good at reading my thoughts because I really didn't understand where she was coming from.

"I don't know how to explain it. He's not the same boy I used to know and could read so well. Well . . . he's a man, now, but my instincts tell me something is bothering him. Something on his mind real heavy-like."

"I haven't noticed it," I told her. "No one else has for that matter . . . at least they haven't mentioned it to me. Maybe it's part of getting acclimated again from being locked up. I ain't never been inside, but I hear it's not an easy thing to do."

"Twenty years he spent. Got caught up in those brand new laws for first-time offenders with drugs. Not even his grandfather with all the power he had could spring him loose. Even though he's finally out of that place I am still going to keep writing my letters to Congress and everyone else who will listen, explaining mandatory sentencing for drug offenses is wrong."

I could see the worry on her face. "So, what kind of changes have you seen in him?"

"He's very quiet. He takes my car at night, drives around for hours like he's searching for something, then back in the house without a word."

"How do you know he's drivin' around all night?"

"I keep records too, West. Every time he gets in and out of the car I write the mileage down . . . Don't know where he's going to and fro— but he's going."

I was careful with my judgment but I just had to add my two cents. "Well, Mrs. Bullock, he has been locked up for twenty years; maybe he's just going out for company."

Her eyes brighten.

"If you know what I mean," I said right before taking in more coffee with the quickness.

"I know what you mean, West, and that type of company should put you sound asleep when you get back home."

She had my complete attention with her truthful wisdom.

"If you know what I . . . mean," she said before she sipped her tea.

I thought about her observations and let Mrs. Bullock know I would keep an eye out for her grandson. It was the least I could do.

Chapter 4

I arrived back at the shop close to lunchtime. The atmosphere was just the way I like it as I walked past the car bays back to my office—busy. All the work being done eased my mind going into the next pay period that I would not have to go into my emergency fund to pay my mechanics. I wasn't purposely seeking out Tavious but I noticed him sitting in his work bay, eating a sandwich and going over paperwork for his next car up, a blue Impala. I didn't want to seem too obvious by going directly over to him and hammering him with his grandmother's concerns, so I decided to speak with him later.

I unlocked the door to my office and Lauren was sitting at my desk, watching the television mounted on my wall. She didn't look my way. It was almost like she was trying to avoid me altogether as I walked in. When I stepped behind my desk to get her out of my seat so I could get to work, I was shocked but pleasantly surprised.

"Baby, are you sitting behind my desk with nothing on?"

"I don't know," she said. Lauren was still looking at the television.

"You don't know? How can you not know?"

She smiled back. Then she placed her hand on the desk, and pushed off so the chair would spin around and reveal her to me entirely. "What's it look like?"

"It looks like you're in here trying to get into some trouble."

"Maybe I am," she said.

I bent down and kissed her on the cheek. "Um, baby, ordinarily I would, but not right now . . . I have to get these checks ready. It's payday."

The sound she made assured me she wasn't happy with my answer, and she pulled me down to her for a hug and a kiss, another hug, and a few more kisses.

"But I promise, baby, I'll make it up to you later."

"You sure?"

"Have I ever let you down?"

Lauren smiled and stood up and grabbed her skirt, wrapped it around her bottom half of her body, and closed it.

I took my chair and placed my papers on my desk and she stood behind me running her fingers down my neck making it very hard for me to concentrate. "Let me ask you something."

"What is it, babe?"

"Tavious."

"The new guy?"

"Yeah."

"What about him?"

"You noticed anything going on with him?"

"Other than he looks a little like that guy Idris Elba, no. Baby, can you imagine someone looking so much like a movie star? I mean it's crazy. I once knew a girl in school named Kelly Kelly and for the life of me I couldn't figure out what the hell was going on with that, but, hey, such is life."

I needed to keep Lauren focused, before she started going off on one of her tangents about any- and everything that comes to her mind. "No, babe, I'm talking about anything strange. Other than his looks," I cleared up.

"Oh his looks ain't strange, believe me when I tell you that."

"Lauren?" I repeated.

"Um, um strange like what?"

"Anything?"

"No, only that he comes in, does his work, and leaves without saying much. Why you ask?"

"I spoke with Mrs. Bullock today and she seems to think her grandson is having some problems with something."

"Problems?"

"Yeah, but she doesn't have any idea of what it could be and she asked me to check into it."

"Well, maybe you should. Maybe he needs someone to talk to . . . Maybe being out is stressing him out."

"Yeah, maybe I will."

With just that little bit of advice from Lauren I was reminded of how good things had been between us. We had been steady like a ship in the ocean, which made our relationship very good to me. She was always there for me without having anyone influence what we had going on, and I tried my best to always be there for her and I was working on getting better.

I finished with payroll, signed the checks for all four of my mechanics, then prepared a deposit for Lauren's bank run. I noticed Tavious walk out of the working bay of the garage but still looking at the car he had up. Most of my mechanics would go outside for a smoke break, use the cell or shoot the shit. So I went out with his paycheck in hand.

As I walked toward Tavious he noticed me and threw his smoke on the ground, smashed it into the ground with his leather work boot, then acknowledged me, sounding as though I were a prison guard ready to take him back to lockup.

"What's good, boss?"

"Not much," I had to yell as we were overtaken in a matter of seconds by the screams of two young boys on motorcycles with straight-open pipes zooming down the street. We watched them as far as our eyes could see.

"Fuckin' crazy-ass fools," Tavious says. "Man, these young boys out here in these streets today are straight crazy, man," he testified.

I smiled and handed him his check. "No doubt. It's going to take you some time to get used to it. Just wait until those fools roll up on you on the freeway roaring with those cut-off pipes."

Tavious swiped his face, pulled out another smoke, and lit it. "You know when I was locked up, you hear a lot about what's going on in these streets from the fresh fish coming in and out— but until you finally see it for yourself it's all just speculation. Shit, the way things are out here, they could have probably embellished a bit more."

I was still looking in the direction of the bikers. "Yeah, those boys probably getting ready to get on I-285 and scare the patience outta some people."

Tavious nodded his head in amazement then looked at his check.

"It's all there right?" I made sure.

"Yeah, it's all good . . . thanks." He looked up from his check. "So, my Grands talked to you about me . . . right?"

His accusation made me think it was painted on my face.

"Yeah, I knew she would."

There was no better segue. "Well, yeah, she did. She's worried about you . . . wondered if I noticed any change in you."

"What'd you say?"

"Told her I haven't, but everything's cool, right?"

Tavious didn't answer right back. He just puffed on his smoke. "My Grands told me that you really helped her out a few years back with some real gangster-like situation."

"Is that right?"

"She didn't tell me the details, but she told me enough to know you got some skills to get things done."

I was glad to hear that. I'd tried to forget about the whole ordeal myself because I almost got Lauren killed behind it all. But I was sure Mrs. Bullock didn't give out any real details.

"She told me that you have the knack for finding things out. Sort of like a private detective without any credentials."

"Geez, I wouldn't go that far." I had to chuckle at her assessment. "I just own a car repair shop . . . That's what I do."

"I hear you, West," he said. "But one thing I've learned in prison is to trust your instincts . . . those guts, man. If you don't, you'll find yourself laid out somewhere with no one to help. But you trust that feeling inside and it will keep you alive until the man upstairs has your place ready for you."

"No doubt about it," I said back.

We were at a quick pause. I was coming close to letting Tavious know that if he had anything on his mind to not hesitate to come see me. Tavious in the meantime was in the middle of a hard, long draw on a fresh smoke. He threw it to the ground, exhaled, then said, "I lost two million dollars, West, and I need you to help me find it."

Chapter 5

Later that night, after eating the delicious meal Lauren had prepared for dinner—it was baked chicken, cabbage, and sweet cornbread, with a cherry-topped cheesecake for dessert—I grabbed my jacket so I could go finish the conversation I was having with Tavious. He told me there was something he wanted to show me and was unable to tell me at the shop, because our conversation was cut short by the two wreckers lugging in two cars, both with transmission issues.

When she first heard of my plans, Lauren wasn't very happy about me wanting to venture out into the streets, as I still hadn't taken care of her needs and she was ready. She even had on a red baby-doll to insinuate the type of night she was expecting. I kissed her on the cheek and promised her that all would be well when I returned, and she assured me things were okay when she put a smile on her face, and that is exactly the reason we were together.

I drove over to Mrs. Bullock's to pick Tavious up. As soon as he got in the car, he looked around inside and told me that he remembered when his grandfather used to drive him around in it. Then he began to give me directions on where we were going, which took us about twenty minutes to get to.

I parked my car on a borderline creepy street in a residential neighborhood that had only one working, dim streetlight. There was no hiding the fact that the economic downturn was affecting the neighborhood as we passed a few homes that looked as though they had been boarded up for quite some time. Tavious pointed to an old-time colonial-looking number. I stopped the car and parked across the street from it. Through the darkness, this house didn't look nearly as bad as the others. My eyes had to venture past a few stragglers who were walking down the street and had a brown paper bag in rotation as they moved about to their destination.

I looked up at the house. As much as I could see, it was painted white with black trim, with trees between the two houses that sat to either side of it. I turned to Tavious in the car. "So, what's so special about this place?"

Tavious rolled his window down all the way. "It's where my money is," he said.

I looked back at the house again. I couldn't tell if anyone was home because there was just one light on outside by the porch. "Who lives there?" I asked him.

"Friend," Tavious shot back.

"Friend got a name?"

"Amara, her name is Amara." Tavious then lit up a smoke.

"Doesn't look like she's home to me," I told him.

"Oh, she's there. She's there," Tavious said, without saying anything else.

After a few minutes of looking up at the house in silence I asked him, "So, what is this friend to you, and why does she have your money?"

"We go way back," he said. "Known her since we were eighteen, nineteen years old. She was my right hand when I was deep into the drug game, man. I could trust her with my life," Tavious remembered.

I didn't respond, because it seemed as though Tavious wanted to open up about something, and I thought the sooner he did it would be better for both of us so I could get back to Lauren. There was no doubt in my mind she would be waiting for me as soon as I hit the door.

"There wasn't a time that I didn't trust her," Tavious mentions.

"That good of a friend, huh?"

"Yeah, the best," he said. "All the way up to me getting snagged on that possession charge that got me that twenty-year bid."

Mrs. Bullock never did explain the details of his drug charge conviction and I often wondered what the whole deal was about. I knew for a fact that Tavious wasn't a killer because she told me that much, but the twenty-year sentence that he endured always did give me pause. "So, how'd you end up doing twenty?" I asked him. There was still no type of movement in the house.

"Found with over sixty pounds of weed on me, coming back from Miami," he said. "But what did me in was the Feds. They waited until I was right in front of a school around the corner from my spot to pull me over. Got me with intent to distribute within a thousand yards of a school on a Saturday night, around two in the morning," he reflected. "The only good thing about that night was that Amara went with me to Miami to pick up our money and re-up. We decided to split up and ride different buses back here. Her duffle bag was the one packed with the two million dollars," he explained.

Things were beginning to make sense to me. "So, you did twenty locked up knowing you had two million out on the streets waiting for you?"

Tavious shook his head yes.

"And how long you been out?"

"Damn near three months," he said.

"Well, if this Amara is such a good friend, why don't you just knock on the door and get it?"

Tavious looked at the house, then took a swipe at his face, then looked at me. "'Cause she's dead, man. She's inside that house, dead."

Chapter 6

When I heard the word "dead" I sat up from underneath the wheel of the car, looked up the street, then into my rearview mirrors for any sign of the police. In my world, a corpse in a house means nothing but police. "What do you mean, dead?"

"Dead, man. Amara's in that house dead," he made clear.

Fuckin' unbelievable what I was hearing from Tavious. I got out my car and looked behind it and down the street as far as I could see without any reflective help. Tavious even asked me what I was doing. When I was sure not a soul was watching the house or us, I got back into the car. "How do you know she's dead?"

Tavious exhaled to a point where I knew he didn't want to explain. "Look, when I first got out of the pen, after I got something to eat, this was my first stop. I knocked on the door, waited—no answer. So I walked in. I looked around the house and found her inside. Her body was still warm."

I just about had my bearings back. I asked him, "You sure she was dead?"

Tavious looked at me stern. "I'm sure, man, she was dead. Not moving, not breathing, dead, man. Blood was everywhere." He paused. "I only looked around for a while, I couldn't stand being in there with her like that."

I took a long, investigative glance at the house and blurted out to Tavious that I didn't see any police tape around any of the doors, or signs that anyone knew she was dead.

"Nobody knows yet," Tavious responds.

"Only the person who killed her," I said back, then looked directly at Tavious and he got my drift.

"Aww, hell no, man, I didn't do it." He couldn't tell by my looks if I believed him. "C'mon now . . . West. Why would I come back here if I killed her? That would mean I'd have my money, and if I had it, I wouldn't have told you about it in the first place."

I looked at him longer this time through the darkness and that damn dim streetlight. He looked back at me just as stern. "Yeah, I guess," I decided.

"Got-damn right," he mumbled.

We sat and looked at the house for another hour or so without a word. I thought that if her dead body had been in that house for three months the sight and smell would be unbearable. There was still no movement on the street. Nothing from across the street; next door everything completely still.

"There's no one around," Tavious said. "I can assure you of that."

"Makes you so sure?"

"Because . . . I've been out here every night since I found her. Damn house has pulled me here every night, like some kind of magical magnet or some shit. Rest on my word, nobody knows."

"Except the person who killed her," I reminded him.

Chapter 7

The only reason I didn't put my car in drive with the velocity of an Indy car driver, drop Tavious off, and tell him to forget he ever told me about his dead friend was because I thought about Mrs. Bullock and her confirmation to me that Tavious had been leaving the house every night and hanging out for hours at a time. Her suspicions gave him an alibi for the time being and as we sat in the car he propositioned me with an offer that would make any man ponder.

"West, if fifty thousand is not enough then, fuck it, name your price," Tavious had pushed for the second time in less than thirty seconds.

I looked at the house again and took a deep, long breath, then told Tavious that I brought him out to the house only as a favor. Just to listen to him, to see where his head was at because I promised his grandmother I would. I let him know my intentions were not to get involved with a murder or his twenty-year-old dirty drug money.

"Ohh . . . I get it," he said. Tavious's tone was completely different now and I even noticed him tapping his foot on the floor of the car in frustration. "You think I'm some kind of halfway-reformed thug who hasn't learned his lesson after twenty years behind bars, don't you?"

I didn't answer him because before I could say anything Tavious began talking again.

"I have my degree, West. In math and sociology, do you have yours?" he challenged.

"Nah, never been much for studying outside car schematics and manuals," I let him know.

"Well, not that it means much either way. I'm just saying. I have mine and it doesn't mean a damn thing because who's going to hire me anyway even with the paper?"

"Well, I hired you," I told him.

"Yeah, you did and I appreciate that. But beyond your shop, who's going to give me a chance once they see that I did twenty?" Tavious exhaled. "Man, I was a straight A student all the way through school. I didn't even know what a letter grade of B looked like on a report card when I was coming up. I had scholarship offers, and not for playing sports but for my grades. Name a university and I can crawl up in my grandmother's attic and show you a letter from the college offering me a full-ride academic scholarship. But guess what, West?"

Once again, he didn't give me a chance to get a word in. In addition to that, I was still thinking about his academic success. I gained a different view of him.

"I was too smart for my own good," he said. "I met the wrong group of people, stand-up people by society's standards, who showed me a process on how the drug game worked, and I used my brain to build the largest marijuana cartel that this city has ever seen." He paused and swiped his face. "And now, I'm back on the streets as a free man for the first time since becoming a convicted man, with the only friend I've really known lying up in that house because of the money she was holding for me."

A potential dead body in the house and Tavious going a mile a minute about his life had me perplexed and thinking about too many things at one time. I had been at his point of frustration before and I just allowed him to vent. There was absolutely nothing that I could say to him because we had lived two entirely different lives: his in captivity and mine as a free man, trying to never go where he had been. What he said to me did connect. I personally knew how difficult it was trying to get the start-up capital for my business and to sustain what I had, and I understood completely the lack of faith to become anything but an ex-con. More than that, I'd always envisioned myself going where he just came out of. Sort of like an engraved destination that hadn't materialized in reality by the grace of God.

For minutes no other words were spoken between us. We just sat and watched the house. I could hear Tavious mumble something about his friend Amara a few times under his breath but instead of asking him about it, I just let it pass; then I hear him burble a few times more in the darkness. It wasn't without fail that I thought how I would react if Lauren was inside a house, dead after being a rock for me for over twenty years. The notion of it all made me step up.

"So, let's just say I agree to go in there with you." I almost ate my words when Tavious turned to me so rapidly with hope in his eyes. I put my hand up to let him know that I wasn't finished. "And if I do, we do it my way. That's the only way I'll go in there, Tavious . . . we do it my way."

I could see Tavious's craving through the darkness. "Yeah, I can live with that," he said. "I hear you're good at what you do anyway," he said, as I sensed he was getting himself psyched to get back in that house.

"I'm good at running my shop," I wanted to let him know.

He snickered, dismissing me a bit. "Yeah, I know. Well if my money is in that house, I hope you can live with a hundred thousand cash, because what you're doing, man, means a lot," he said. "Let's go."

Chapter 8

With not a lot more said, other than how we were going to get in and out of the house, we made our way. I parked around the corner away from the house. Then we walked around back toward the house passing the same crew of fellows drinking who we noticed earlier. They were getting ready to shoot a game of 7-11 on the corner under a brighter streetlight. I was pretty sure they weren't paying us any attention but we watched our backs as we made our way, just in case.

The front door was locked, just like Tavious said it would be because he'd locked it, and we had to get in through a window on the side. I carried a shop rag in with me and used it to push the window up. I followed Tavious in and we walked directly upstairs and there it was: the body and the awful rotten-egg smell that only came from a dead body that had started its intrinsic breakdown.

"See, what did I tell you?" Tavious said. He took one quick glance at Amara, then turned around, not being able to look at her any longer. Her hair was detached from her body. The closest we could get to the body because of the stench was only a few feet.

I could see a stain next to her head; I guessed blood. "No doubt, she's dead all right."

Tavious nodded his head in agreement then walked away from her body. I think he was even crying and I noticed him cover his nose with his shirt as he kicked at the floor.

I moved away from her body and looked around. "Did you touch anything in here besides that doorknob when you locked the door, and that window down there?"

He looked back at me. "Nah, man . . . ."

"Well, don't," I told him. I was already getting paranoid and it was sort of a rush—like the time when my newfound friend Rossi walked into a high-ranking police officer's home to see what we could find a few years back when I caught jury duty.

I went down the steps, wiped the doorknob off with my rag, and made a mental note to wipe down the window when we left. Tavious had no idea where his friend Amara could have hidden the money. After all the years on the inside he never wanted her to tell him because of the taped phone conversations and monitored mail that occurred. We began to look around for it. We searched every place one might think to hide two million cash, and whoever was there before us did too. The house had been made a wreck. The couches, her bed, cabinets, everything turned upside down and searched inside out. Tavious recalled that he didn't remember the house being in that condition, but guessed it could have been because he was half out his mind with Amara being dead and him just being out of prison.

We went over the entire house and didn't find a dime. On the way back down from the second floor I noticed a picture slightly tilted in the stairwell. I looked behind it and there was an opening through the sheetrock with a space that just might have held two million.

"Well, this looks like a good place to hide two million dollars if you ask me," I mentioned to Tavious as he joined me on the steps.

Tavious moved the picture and looked at the space, then reached inside. He pulled out two duffle bags that were completely empty and showed them to me. "These are the bags, man. These are the bags I placed the two million cash in," he said. "Amara told me she never touched it. Always made me feel so good when she told me that I was the last one to ever touch these bags. Now they're gone. I want my fuckin' money, West," he said, as he crumbled the bags up and put them under his arm. "Not only for me, but for Amara, too.

Chapter 9

Looking around for two million while a woman lay dead in her house was as taxing as an eighteen-hour workday. We were back in the car and I suggested a few cold beers on me, at a tiny neighborhood corner bar, but Tavious balked at the idea. He'd grown tired of small places. I completely understood. Instead, he had me pull the car over at a gas station and he walked out with a six that we proceeded to drink in the parking lot of my shop.

"I hated seeing her up in there like that," Tavious uttered right after he cracked open his can. "I've known her for over twenty years and didn't even get to see Amara as a free man again. I can see someone stealing the money. But killing her? What's that about?"

"Maybe someone else thought she was still in the game," I let him know.

"Guess so," Tavious answered, but it didn't sound like he believed it.

"Cared for her a lot, huh?"

"Basically all I had, man. Always took my calls, she always made sure my account was full. Made sure I kept my head clear to do the twenty, man . . . Yeah, she was always there. Really the only family I got besides Grands."

"And if you ever wondered, she loves you too," I let him know. "And I love her," I made clear.

He smiled. "Yeah, she does. I was so pissed at myself that I had let her down when I got popped," Tavious reflected.

I asked him, "What about the rest of your family?"

Tavious paused. He took a long swig of brew, put the empty in the bag, grabbed another, then popped it open and drank half of that. "I never knew my dad. I don't think my mom did either." He laughed it off. "And my mother left Atlanta when I got locked up."

"Left?"

"Yeah, it wasn't without warning either. She always told me—when she had an idea I'd gotten into the game—told me if I got caught, she was leaving and never returning. And I hear it's exactly what she did. Grands said when she found out that I'd gotten arrested she packed her bags and left, and we haven't heard from her since."

I had to take a swig of my brew after that bit of information. "Wow, you haven't seen her since you went in twenty years ago?"

"Nah, man, I haven't seen her since she cooked breakfast for me that morning. Not even a letter. When she found out I got arrested, I took her for her word that she wasn't coming to see me and that she was leaving town. My mom hated what I did and wasn't going to deal, man, not going to even do it—she swore to it."

"That's some tough love."

"Or no love. Depends on how you look at it."

All of a sudden the parking lot is overcome by an awful rattling banging noise that sounds like it's on top of my ride. It shocks Tavious so much he spills some brew on his shirt. I look toward my left and a car is passing, going about three miles an hour, and honestly thinking the shit coming from his trunk is appealing for all to hear.

Tavious throws his empty can of beer in the bag again, then reaches for another. "I been inside all these years and that shit there—with the music, man . . . now, that's some bullshit."

I laugh. "You sound like an old man," I tell him.

Tavious thought a minute. "I guess I do, but I still feel twenty. All this out here is different, man. Being on the inside then coming out fuckin' crazy. These fools out here don't care about who they inconvenience."

"Don't worry, you'll get used to it."

"I guess," he said.

"You have any idea who would have done your girl like that?"

Tavious kept his eyes on his beer can. "Nah. She didn't roll with too many because of the fact she had the money stashed and, as far as I know, she didn't have a man running in and out of there; although I'm sure she had someone coming through from time to time." Tavious turns and looks at me like he didn't even want to imagine that scenario for whatever reason.

"Well, whoever went through that house knew what they were looking for."

"And they found it, and walking around with something I've waited twenty years to get my hands on."

"So, your plan was to work in the shop with your pockets full, without putting any attention on yourself?"

Tavious kind of smiled. "Yeah, that was it. Not initially, but when my old lady came to me weeks before I was released and said you would be willing to let me work at your shop, it became the plan."

"Not a bad plan," I let him know.

There was a pause so strange it made me look at Tavious.

"Well, I'm thinking you can help me with this new one," he said.

Chapter 10

I've been in the predicament of coming home late after a few beers before with my lady waiting on me, anticipating a night of romance, but it wasn't Lauren. It was right before I gave the nod to delve into the monster of a scheme Lauren cooked up while on jury duty when we first met. That night with my ex ended badly, but I was determined not to let it happen the same way, so as soon as I opened the door, I was willing and ready to keep the peace.

When I walked inside the house Lauren was standing in the foyer, still wearing the baby-doll. "Hey, baby," she said.

I stood still, captivated by how good she looked and shocked that I'd only taken one step inside. It was so very similar and eerie to my experience with my ex.

"How's everything?" she wanted to know without a hint of being upset with me.

Very cautiously I told her things were good.

"Want something else to drink? I can get you another beer, if you like."

I still hadn't moved because familiarity with the situation told me it was some kind of set-up. Lauren smiled, turned away, and sashayed into the kitchen, and I followed her feeling like an ox before slaughter.

I stopped at the kitchen island and admired our marble top I'd bartered to get from a remodeler whose company trucks needed work. I watched as she bent over nice and slow into the fridge, pulling out a beer. She walked over to the sink, rinsed the top off, then popped the can open and poured it into my favorite glass, then set it down in front of me.

If she was trying to confuse me she had accomplished her mission, as I stood there wondering if I should take a sip of my beer. I couldn't tell if she was upset with me. I had never stayed out later than expected without giving her a call.

She smiled. "You okay?"

I smiled back, paused, then said, "Yes . . . are you?"

"I'm fine, silly . . . why wouldn't I be?"

In my mind it was another trick so I didn't say anything. I picked up my glass, gave her a confirming smile of gratitude, drank some of the beer, and smiled at her again.

"So, did you find out if anything was bothering Tavious?"

Over the few years Lauren and I had been together I could truly say our relationship was built on trust. At one point in time I thought she wanted marriage, so I asked for her hand, but she surprised me and said she would be okay with the title of lifetime partner, as long as it was loving and trustworthy. I was taken aback by it a bit. But after she sat down with me and I actually got her point of view on the marriage statistics, looking at it I had to agree. Love and commitment is love and commitment, paper or not.

But tonight, I had walked up on a murder, a gruesome murder of a good friend of a former drug kingpin who was fresh out the penitentiary. No, I was not letting that speck of info into our atmosphere, because I didn't know how it happened and I damn sure didn't want to involve Lauren, no matter how street smart she was.

"He's just having a bit of anxiety with trying to get adjusted back to society and all," I let her know.

"Is he going to be all right? He's not thinking of doing anything that will get him put back in, is he?"

"No, he'll be fine. He needed someone to listen to him vent. There is so much to the penal system that I wasn't aware of, babe."

Lauren smiled and then placed a wondrous look on her face. I asked if she was okay, right before I took in more beer.

"Yes, I'm fine."

"You sure are," I let her know. "Is that baby-doll for me?"

"If you want it to be . . . I mean if you're not too tired from being out tonight."

"No way. Didn't I promise I would take care of you?"

Lauren snuggled up against me. "Sure did . . ."

Chapter 11

Back at the shop it had been jumping busy for the past three days and we were one mechanic short and that tech just happened to be Tavious. I hadn't seen nor heard from him since the night we saw Amara's dead body. That first day back to work he missed was completely understandable. The second day I was a little annoyed because he didn't call, but I still understood. His friend was dead. On the third day, I at least expected a call from him to let me know his plans for the rest of the week so I could make scheduling changes, or even give some work to a mechanic or two who I knew were out of work. But, I held out and found myself working in his bay, changing a catalytic converter for a woman who thought the process should take five minutes to complete.

I hadn't called Mrs. Bullock to see if things were okay. But I promised myself it was next on my to-do list. I was standing checking the connections under the 2002 Volvo converter and a voice came from behind the front right wheel of the car.

"That thing on tight?"

I turned to look behind me; it was Tavious. I gave him a long gaze. "Yeah, she's ready to roll. 'Bout to drop her down now."

Tavious moved closer for a bit more privacy. "Look, West . . . I know I should have called in but . . ."

I had cooled a bit after finishing the job. There was no way I was going to even begin to think I understood the feelings coming from this man who had been waiting to see someone for over twenty years, then when he finally got a chance to see her she was dead. Besides, I needed to get my hands dirty for old time's sake anyway. It reminded me of when my garage was on the curb in front of my house. I thumped Tavious on the shoulder and just asked him if he was okay. He looked tired and a bit worried. No doubt the two million and the death of his friend were lying hard on him. He was far from the bright-eyed man Mrs. Bullock brought in on his first day to meet me. When I first laid eyes on him my initial thoughts were that he was nowhere near reaching into his forties because his body had been well maintained. But now he looked in need of some good news and worry-free rest.

I walked over to the entrance of the bay, hit the switch so the Volvo could touch the ground, and I motioned Tavious over to me. "Look, while you were out, I had a chance to think about what this place needs around here to get it clicking the way I want it. And I thought about you."

"Me?"

"Yes, you."

"What, you've come up with a plan to help me get my money?"

I kind of chuckled. "Oh yeah, that . . . I don't think so, Tavious. Whoever has your money is probably more of a problem than I want to deal with."

Tavious took a deep breath and looked away from me.

"But what I did decide was to make you in charge of my lean program."

"Lean what?"

"Lean program. It's a process program on how to get these guys around here to work smarter and stop wasting so much material and shit."

Tavious looked at me with distaste and confusion.

"Don't worry about it . . . you'll understand more when I get all the information to you."

"But—"

"Don't worry about it. If it's more money you want, consider it done. I just think with being locked up all those years, you have a lot of experience with working with what you have, and keeping things in order. I don't know if you noticed, but I listened to you the night we were in the car. I heard what you said about how difficult it is for felons—"

Tavious interrupted me. "Nonviolent, West."

"My mistake, nonviolent criminals, to come back into society and get work. So what I want to do is get you more involved around here. Doing more than just working on the cars. I am going to give you more responsibility, so one day if you want, you can get your own shop or even run the next one I open up."

"Look, I don't have time for that, West. I need to get my money," he said back to me, almost chuckling.

"Don't worry about it. Come to the office a little later and I will give you all the info I have on getting this place into shape."

We were standing eye to eye now. I was expecting Tavious to show some type of excitement; after all, I was putting into place something he said didn't exist. But all I got was a blank stare and a pat on the back. Then he told me thank you and walked back to the locker room to get ready for work.

Chapter 12

I went back to my office and sat behind my desk to take a breather. It had been much too long since I'd been under a car. I circled the next Tuesday coming on my calendar to make it a point to go at it again, to keep my skills sharp. My eyes traveled along my desk to a note I wrote myself to call Mrs. Bullock. Initially it was to check on Tavious, but my call this time would be to tell her that I hadn't seen a change in him and in my estimation he was okay, just so she wouldn't worry. He still had his mind set on getting that money. But I didn't want to bother Mrs. Bullock with any unnecessary chat about a dead body and millions of dollars that disappeared that Tavious wanted. That alone would more than likely put old girl in stroke status. Hopefully, Tavious would just let things blow over.

I made the call to Mrs. Bullock, assured her everything was okay; then I kicked back in my chair, put my feet up on my desk, and fell asleep for what seemed like two seconds before I was awakened by my feet being pushed off my desk. Two men now standing in my office were looking over me.

"Are you West Owens?" one of them demanded as I struggled to get my bearings.

"Yeah, I'm West. Who the fuck are you?"

One of the men looked over at the other and smiled, then said, "Police," in a deep baritone voice. He took a few steps closer and proceeded to knock some of the papers I had on my desk to the floor; then he sat down on my desk like he owned it.

Police or not, I didn't like the fact that he had the nerve to put his hands on me nor stand in my shop and act like he was in control of everything inside it. I stood up to show my displeasure. "Look, I don't know who or what you guys want, but I do know you're going to respect my place of business."

The smirks on their faces let me know they had heard my spiel before. These were young cats. The white one was razor-sharp bald and somewhat familiar, so I kept my eye on him the most. He looked like his bed was probably in the middle of a gym someplace, and he was in need of a tailor who could extend his fabric on his suit so he could breathe. The black one was a little taller, leaner, with a haircut like a marine Mr. T style with beady eyes. He was the one who slapped at my feet and would be the one I would have chosen to knock out if someone put their hand on me again. At that moment I could tell my distain for the police had not subsided since my run-in with Captain Stallings of the Atlanta Police Department. I just couldn't tolerate how they did business.

"Off the desk," I told him.

He couldn't have moved from my desk any slower as he asked, "So, you're West Owens?" The black one wanted to know.

"Did the barber cut your ears off, too?" I asked him.

His partner put his head down and smiled. That's when I realized who he was. He worked with Stallings and was the cop who pulled me over in my car, pounded me in the face, and took me to the abandoned house when I was on jury duty.

"You're right, he is a handful, Gus," the black cop, whose nametag read WILLIAMS, blurted out.

I turned to Gus. "Oh, so you seem to think you know me, Gus? What do you guys want?"

"We want to talk to Tavious Bell. Does he work here?"

"I might have to look through all this paperwork in these files to tell you that. You guys want to wait?" Gus was plain and clear. "If it takes you too long, I could go see Mrs. Bullock and ask her," he said.

Tavious opened my door and poked his head inside. "You page me on the intercom, boss? I already told you, man, I'm going to have to pass on that lean shit."

I motioned to the cops, and when he saw them he brushed his shirt off, then stepped inside but didn't say a word. "Tavious, these police officers came to see you—" I let him know.

Williams interrupted. "We didn't ask you to introduce us," he said to me. Then he looked hard at Tavious. "Tavious Bell?"

Tavious looked at him, his eyes a bit wider now; then he looked over at Gus, who looked way too uncomfortable standing in one spot. "Yeah, that's me. What's this about?"

"You tell me," Gus pushed.

I was about tired of this guy. "Look, if you want to see him, there he is. Stop with the bullshit."

"What's going on, West?" Tavious wondered.

"I'm Detective Williams, APD."

"Okay . . ." Tavious listened.

"Do you know Amara Sullivan?"

"Uh, no, no . . . Yeah, I know her . . . Why?"

"Just a question," Williams said.

"When was the last time you saw her?" Gus was matter-of-fact.

"Uh, I don't know, it's been awhile . . . I just did a twenty-year bid."

I had to interrupt because Tavious was beginning to sweat and I didn't like the way he began to squirm and show his uneasiness. "Look, why are you guys here?"

"Because we are," Gus said.

"What's your job here?" Williams wanted to know.

"I'm a mechanic."

Gus prodded, "A mechanic?" Then he chuckled.

"No, he's my lean manager, for my shop," I injected.

"Lean manager?" Williams asked.

"Don't worry about it. I got a feeling you wouldn't understand," I told him.

"You know Amara's dead right?" Gus shot off with quickness, trying to catch a reaction.

Tavious looked at me, and the detectives were following his every move. "No, no, I didn't know that."

"Now you do," Williams said. Then he tapped Gus on the shoulder and pointed to the door, but before they walked out Williams turned. "Who's your parole officer, Bell?"

Tavious told him his parole officer's name, then let the officer know he was finished with his probation and was a free man. The cops walked out without another word.

I motioned to Tavious not to say a word until I followed the cops with my eyes through my window until they were off the lot. "Okay, they're gone," I verified.

Tavious was already sitting in a chair across from my desk. I waited for him to say something but he didn't. "Hey, man, you all right?"

Tavious was clearly shaken and looked as though he was in pain. I sat down in my chair and took a long, deep breath the way Lauren begs me to do throughout my day, then reached down, opened my cabinet, and took out a bottle of whiskey with two glasses. I opened the bottle and poured. Still not a word from Tavious. When I went over to give him his glass, I had to put it in his hand. I was already on my second glass when he finally took a sip and spoke.

"What the fuck am I drinking?" he said.

"Whiskey. It will bring you back," I told him.

He looked at his glass. "Whiskey?"

"What's wrong, you never had it?"

"West, I got locked up before I was twenty." He took a sip and dealt with the burn. "And got-damn it, it looks like they're going to put me right back in there." Tavious took his glass all the way back and I walked over and filled him up again.

I sat back down at my desk. "Well it's evident they have found her body and know you two were in contact."

"But how?" Tavious exploded.

"A letter, her phone bill, anything could have triggered that. The technology they have these days will make your head spin, man; you have to be careful."

A few minutes had passed and Tavious was now slouched down in his chair, holding the glass, looking up at the ceiling. "All they have to do is think I did it, West. That's all they have to do and I won't have a chance. Plus, I'm an ex-con. Shit, they'll probably put a charge on me then have me on death row like they did Troy Davis. I haven't even been out six months and I have a case on me already. How'd they even find out she was dead?"

I didn't know what to say to Tavious. The way the cops were eyeballing him there was no way in hell I was going to tell him they weren't interested in him concerning the murder, and Tavious picked up on my silence.

He sat up in his chair and pointed at me with his glass. "Look at you, you're even lost for words. I'm an easy collar, man. Fresh out of prison, evidence of contact with Amara . . . Hell they don't need nothing else to make up a story and tell twelve fuckin' jurors that I killed her, and it would be their word against mine." He paused. "Have you ever heard a man cry because he lost his freedom, West?"

I took a sip of my drink while looking at Tavious over the top of my glass, and shook my head no.

"It's the worst sound in the world, man. Hearing a man cry who is locked up and can't do a thing about it but cry is a terrible thing, man; nobody should have to listen to that type of bellow."

All of a sudden Tavious was silent and he knocked back what was left in his glass. I locked eyes with Tavious and he knew that I knew he was right. They were about to do him. It was only a matter of time before they pulled him in for questioning.

"You have to help me, man, you know I didn't kill her . . . You got to help me."

Chapter 13

Lauren was a gem. I had only mentioned to her in conversation how much I missed a straight-edge shave from the barber since by law they were no longer allowed to give them because of blood issues. Like magic she appeared with her razor from cosmetology school. She had hot towels and shaving cream to take care of me with a nice shave. But I just had to remove one of the towels she put on my face and open my eyes.

"Are you sure you know what you're doing, babe?"

"Yes, I know," she said, almost sounding cocky.

"Okay . . . but that razor looks awfully sharp," I said.

"West, would you hush up? How is a straight-edge supposed to look? Did you give your barber so much chitchat about his razor?"

"He was my barber though."

"And I'm your lady. I wouldn't let anything happen to you, now sit back and enjoy, babe."

I did and Lauren put me at ease in no time at all. The steaming hot towels were heaven and I was nice and relaxed, so tranquil that I told her about Tavious and the visit from the police at the shop.

"Now, West, baby, don't answer me because you will mess up the shave, but I want you to listen to me a minute, okay? I'll take your not saying anything as affirmation," she said.

Lauren started shaving the left side of my face. I could tell she was concentrating on doing a good job.

As she took care of my face, Lauren let me know that she thought I should help Tavious anyway that I could. I appreciated Lauren's support because it was the only reason I hadn't gone out to the streets with Tavious to find out who murdered his friend. I wanted to honor my word that I had given her to keep the APD out of our lives and leave detective work to actual detectives. Lauren lost her child the last time I got involved unraveling a situation and I did not want to do anything to disrespect that memory.

A few minutes after Lauren finished my shave I called Tavious. I let him know that I would do whatever I could to help him find out who killed Amara before the police moved in on him.

Chapter 14

One thing about Lauren: if I was in something so was she. Out of curiosity she did an Internet search on Amara and was surprised to see an article about her murder. The article didn't say much other than her place was ransacked, her body badly decomposed, and the police were on the hunt. The funeral services happened to be the very next day after reading the article. I called Tavious and let him know that I would tag along with him if he wanted to pay his last respects, which I felt was a good idea.

We were in my ride on our way to Amara's funeral. I decided while we were there it would be a good idea to try to get any information possible that might help us find out what happened to her. Tavious didn't recall ever meeting any of her family. He remembered that she would sometimes chat about them when he would call her collect from the inside. It was going to take us about twenty minutes to get to our destination.

"So, you mean to tell me my grandmother gave you this car?" Tavious asked for at least the third time, referring to my mint-condition vintage El Camino we were rolling in.

I just smiled and wiped down her dash, then turned up the radio a few clicks.

"I remember my grandfather taking me to the store to get candy in this thing." Tavious paused. "Oh my goodness that's my song . . . That's . . ." He snapped his fingers over and over, trying to remember.

"Phyllis Hyman," I tell him.

"Whatever happened to her?"

"They say suicide," I let him know.

Tavious was blunt. "You damn sure don't hear any Phyllis Hyman in the joint, that's for sure."

The obituary in the paper read that Amara's funeral was at two in the afternoon at Progressive United Church and we arrived a few minutes before. Tavious was a bit hesitant about going inside and stayed back a few minutes to gather his composure while I went inside.

There was a picture on an easel of Amara with sky blue linen fabric draped artistically on the canvas and mellow music playing. I figured by the sound it was neo soul, then recognized Jill Scott's voice because Lauren loved her, and then Anthony Hamilton because I loved him on the song after that. When I walked into the chapel there were about twenty people inside all dressed in white. Some were chatting, others were reading Amara's obituary, and a few were staring at me.

I looked back at the entrance to find out if Tavious had made his way inside. When I turned back around there was a short man standing in front of me. He was giving me the third degree with his eyes over my entire being. He didn't speak. So, I did.

"I'm okay," he answered. "After all, it's a funeral."

I nodded in agreement, noticing his eyes traveling over me some more.

"I see you came dressed for the occasion." He had on a white soft linen shirt, and white pants with white shoes.

I got his point after looking around at everyone again. "Uh, yeah. I didn't get the dress announcement." I had on a black suit and brown shoes.

"Yeah, but she's gone home, man . . . Our people are homegrown from Georgia. We celebrate these types of things," he said. "White," he emphasized."White." I got it. I swear I did, but the more I thought about it, I decided it didn't matter what I had on. She was gone and I didn't know her anyway.

The deed of just staring back at this guy was beginning to feel a bit odd. When Tavious met up with me there was a bit of relief. Tavious acknowledged him with a half smile. The man was very light skinned, with freckles, and weighed about 140 pounds. He took even a longer time to look Tavious over before he finally spoke.

He pointed at Tavious. "Wow, man, Amara never told me she knew you," he said. "Tell me how you two met. I always knew she was keeping a secret from me."

Tavious didn't respond.

"I loved the show," the man rushed to say. "You probably hear this all the time, but I was pissed when they killed you off. *The Wire* was such an experience," he said.

Tavious chuckled. "No, no . . . you got it all wrong. I'm not that guy. We just happened to look alike."

"Really?" he asked while he continued his examination of Tavious. "Amazing, man, just freakin' amazing. So, what are you guys, cops? Why are so many of you here, if I may ask? If you ask me, you should be out trying to catch who killed my cousin instead of hanging out here. By the way, my name is Chuck."

"Cops?" We're not cops," Tavious let him know.

Chuck looked us over again. "Who are you then?"

"My name is Tavious and this is West."

We exchanged handshakes and I told Chuck we were sorry for his loss, as he let us know that Amara's mom and his mother were sisters.

"And how did you know Amara?" he wanted to know.

"I've known her for years," Tavious said.

"And I'm just here to support him," I let him know.

Chuck looked us up and down again without another word, then walked away, leaving us standing. We watched him walk from person to person in attendance and nod over to us until the funeral began.

Everyone had so many kind words for Amara. I can truly say she was a shining light in many minds. Chuck even tried to find out how well Tavious really knew Amara by inviting him to say a few words about her. Tavious called his bluff without hesitating, and he let everyone know that she was definitely a superstar who helped him for years make it out of a dark place. Most in attendance gave Tavious a hug, even Chuck afterward.

The funeral ended and we rode in the processional to the burial. Tavious was shaken seeing Amara going home, but he stood strong and tried to put in perspective that she was free and his freedom was at stake.

Chuck let us know that there was going to be food and drink in the city afterward if we were able to join the family. Right before we got into the car to leave the cemetery we were stopped by a man who reminded me at first sight of Chris Rock: slim, dressed nice, with dark skin.

"I just wanted to talk to you guys before you left," he said; then he extended his hand to Tavious. "My name is Earl and I heard what you said at the funeral."

Tavious looked over at me.

"I hung out with Amara a lot. She was probably the closet cousin I've ever had. Your name rang a bell at the funeral because I have been over her house a few times when you would call her on the phone." He paused and smiled. "Collect."

Tavious smiled back. "Yeah, I did that a lot." He was still emotional and swiped at his face.

"I'm just saying, man, she really trusted you, and I'm glad you came."

I felt it was safe to ask our new friend Earl a few questions and I moved in on the chance not long after I introduced myself. "Earl, can you tell us if she was in any trouble?"

He was happy to oblige. "No; she didn't hang out with a lot of people. She was happy being a homebody and once or twice told me she was excited that you were coming back."

"She said that?" Tavious sounded like he might have doubted his words.

"Yeah, more than once . . . I'm sure of it," Earl let him know.

Tavious kind of smiled again.

"So, she wasn't worried or having problems with anyone?" I asked Earl.

"No, but she did talk to a guy named Rodney a lot."

"Rodney?" Tavious wanted to know.

"Yeah, a real interesting character."

"What do you mean?" I asked.

Earl reached into his pocket and gave me a box of matches. "Here, find out for yourself."

Chapter 15

It's close to six now. We were going to call it a day
and start fresh the next sunrise. But Tavious decided
he wanted to keep going. I didn't mind even though I
knew the traffic on I-75 would be a monster. If truth be
told I was becoming more interested by the minute in
what was going on, especially when Earl hinted that we
could find out more from the matchbox he handed over
to us that read TQC. It was located in a high-rise build-
ing in Buckhead. We knew we were pressing our luck
that it would still be open because of the time of day.

The office was on the twenty-eighth floor. A stunning Ethiopian woman greeted us with a smile right
after I noticed her look at her timepiece on her arm.
We asked for Rodney. When we told her we didn't have
an appointment but mentioned Amara, she gave us an
inquiring look. She called Rodney on the phone, then
asked us to sit down and wait. There was nothing in the
office that gave us any inclination of what TQC meant.
So we sat and waited for Rodney and enjoyed the contemporary feel of his office space.

About five minutes later the African princess led us
back to his office where Rodney was finishing a phone
call. He was a well-dressed man, dark skin, athletic. As
he turned to look at us my perception of him was that
he was full of either swagger or shit.

"Hey, I'm Rodney," he said. He placed his phone

down and stood behind his desk and offered us seats. "What can I do for you?" He paused and took a better look at Tavious. "I understand you're friends of Amara. May God rest her soul." There was a pause. "She'll be missed. I hope whoever killed her rots in hell."

"Well, that's what we are trying to see if we can make happen," I let him know.

"What are you guys, cops?"

I shook my head no.

"PI's? What?"

"Friends," Tavious let him know. "I was a good friend of Amara's. My name is Tavious Bell and he's West Owens, a friend of mine."

Rodney puts his index finger on his lip, then points at Tavious. Then he begins to laugh a bit, walks from behind the desk, and extends his hand to Tavious and pats him on the back.

"Tavious . . . You got out? You're finally home," he said. "Damn, I should have known when you walked in the door. She was right, you look just like the guy on *The Wire*. What's his name?" Rodney was in deep trying to remember the movie star's name. "Idris . . ."

"Idris Elba," Tavious helps him out. Tavious turned to me while Rodney had a grip on his hand. Tavious was perplexed and eventually Rodney felt his confusion, then pointed at me.

"Amara talked about this guy all the time." Then he looked down at Tavious, who was sitting in his chair. "I finally get to meet the man."

Tavious pushed, "The man?"

"That's what I heard. No, no, let me put it like this: that's what I always thought." Rodney went into his liquor cabinet and pulled off a bottle of his top shelf. "You . . ." He turned around to us and back at the glasses in the cabinet. "You, my man, definitely had a fan in Amara."

Tavious smiled, but it was more like confusion rather than poking out his chest. I sat and listened, trying to get what I could from Rodney. He displayed a hint of his New York roots by his accent.

"All she did was talk about you were coming home and things were about to change for her," Rodney mentioned to Tavious. "She was even hitting the gym on another level when you were about nine months out. Yeah, she was definitely waiting for you, my brother." Rodney finished pouring the drinks, and handed out the glasses. "Just a shame what happened to her, damn shame."

"That's why we are here," I let him know.

Rodney stopped before he put his glass to his lips. "They find her killer or something?"

Tavious told him no.

"Well, I don't know what I can do to help but if I can, I will." Rodney tilted his head back and took his drink straight down.

"I don't think I saw you at her service," I said.

Rodney gave me a look. "Nah, man. I don't do funerals. If you guys ever hear of me dying, don't even bother looking up my homecoming 'cause it ain't happening," he let us know.

So, we drank. Then drank some more as Rodney was very helpful telling us everything he knew about Amara and how he came into contact with her. He told us that she was actually one of the few people he had met in his business who he could call a friend, even though their friendship was basically relegated to phone conversations. But, even still, he felt he knew her better than most of his clients.

We sat and chatted with Rodney over an hour. TQC

turned out to be a very interesting business venture that Amara patronized on a frequent basis; and Rodney ran it like the multi-million dollar company that it was. It was interesting to learn that he modeled his business from the site that hooks up married people with other likeminded individuals who are looking for affairs. Rodney was sure to let us know that he could never be down with married people cheating on one another, especially after coming from a broken home. But he did say that with over a 50 percent divorce rate he was most eager to help couples keep the spice in their relationships and stay married as long as they could. He called his business entity the Quiver Club. It was an exclusive adult club specializing in voyeurism and relaxation for couples and likeminded singles who respected marriage. Rodney was adamant that his club was for the grown and sexy and that he didn't let anyone under thirty-five join. According to Rodney he met Amara a little over five years ago, a few months after starting his new business venture. Rodney relayed that he would never forget the phone call he received from her, because she had been the only phone call who requested to get information from him over the phone instead of his million-dollar generating Web site, which detailed what his club was all about.

He divulged to us that Amara had been his most particular client. She desired to play within TQC, which provided willing couples who enjoyed the attention of men or woman alike while being intimate with one another. When Tavious heard of her appetite he called Rodney a damn liar and told him he was about to kick his fuckin' ass. Rodney didn't back down but pleaded with him that he was telling the truth. After I settled Tavious down and Rodney poured him another drink, Rodney slowly divulged that Amara was so specific in what she wanted. That it took her almost a year to actually go through with a meeting and enjoying what the club had to offer. He said that she wanted to experience a couple who were actually in love instead of those performing because their lust pushed them to do so.

I wasn't amazed at the TQC setup as Tavious seemed to be after being locked up for over twenty years. But he was even more surprised that Rodney was aware of him and the feelings Amara shared with him concerning Tavious. Out of respect for Amara, Rodney gave us the name of a couple he was sure she had been involved with, and free passes to a meet and greet and told us we should attend. Rodney explained that people in the lifestyle were very close-mouthed when it came to divulging information within the community, let alone to complete strangers, so we would have to tread lightly on how we went about getting information. We assured him his information would be kept confidential.

When I returned home the first thing I did was apologize to Lauren for being late for dinner. She loved to cook and always wanted to serve her food nice and hot. She made an amazing pot roast, with the little red potatoes and green beans. I had asked for seconds before I finally let her know that I was ready to take her out on the date that I'd been promising. I let her know very carefully that I wanted to take her to the Quiver Club as she poured me a second glass of wine.

"A sex club, West?" she asked after I told her what type of place it was.

I procured a sip of my wine. "Yup." Then waited for her next response.

"You want me to go into a club where people meet each other for sex?"

I just knew she was daring me to ask her again, but

the cat was already out the bag. "Yup," I answered
again; then I rushed. "Babe, it's for Tavious. We need
to get to the bottom of this situation because the police
are starting to prowl." I looked at my glass. "Look, do
we have anything stronger than this?"

She put her fork down and reached for her drink. I
was preparing to feel her drink all over my face. But she
took a sip. "Yes, I'll go," she said. Then she got up from
the table. "Would you like a beer, baby?"

I'm bewildered now. I was sure it was probably plas-
tered on my face. I was ready for a heated debate. Some
"how dare you's," some "fool, are you crazy's."

"Sure," she said, with a surprising coy little smile.
"I never said I was a church girl, West, never even
portrayed to be. Who knows, it just might be fun; plus
I hear those type of spots are opening up all over the
country." She opened a can of beer for me, placed it
next to my plate, then sat down and began to finish her
food.

"You hear, huh?" I wanted to know.

"Umm, hmm . . ." she sang.

"From who?"

"A little birdie, babe . . . a tiny little birdie."

"Tomorrow night, at eight," I let her know.

"No worries, I'll be ready."

Chapter 16

By the way she looked, the short-notice invite I gave to Lauren to accompany me to the TQC meet and greet didn't hamper her ability one bit to look stunning. She asked me at least ten times to keep my eyes on the road as we ventured downtown. I just couldn't help myself.

When we arrived at the ballroom of the Ritz my first thoughts were we had run up on a SSOABC (Stuffy-Son-Of-A-Bitch Club) instead of a meet and greet of the unbound and unrestricted minds Rodney said would be in attendance. There were well over 200 people inside. Some sitting, others standing listening to the music or enjoying the all-you-can-eat buffet. We were only inside a few minutes before a waiter walked up to us. He had a tray of nice-looking silver and bluish tinted flutes filled to the brim with champagne. He took our tickets, gave them a quick glance, then gave us champagne in the blue tinted flutes and told us to enjoy ourselves.

Lauren looked around. "They don't look so uninhibited to me, West," Lauren said. "But this champagne is very nice . . ."

About twenty minutes later, the same waiter walked over to us and asked if we were going to enjoy any more of the buffet. I told him no. He asked us to follow him. We followed him out a side door, down a hallway, then out another door into an alley. There was a black sedan waiting on us along with the driver. The driver sped off down the alley, made a right-hand turn, then went into another alley and stopped. The entire trip in the car was about two minutes. The car stopped next to a door. I watched the driver pick up his phone, text something, and the door next to the car opens up. A bulky man appears. He is wearing a suit. He taps his finger on top of the car two times. The driver unlocks the doors of the car. The man in the suit opens the door, extends his hand to Lauren to help her out.

We followed the man in the suit down a long, dark hallway. It was lined with blue lights in contemporary fixtures. We passed four rooms. Two of the doors were open. Both rooms were completely dark inside. I could tell they were occupied but I couldn't see what was going on. In the hallway there was a man standing with a tray of drinks. Lauren took one without missing a stride, then looked at me with bright eyes. Finally, the man leading us stopped and knocked on a huge double door. Another man looked at us and smiled as he extended his arm and invited us inward.

We went inside. After a few steps we were looking toward a huge gathering of people in a gigantic room. To the naked eye they came across as silhouettes because of the lighting setup inside. There was no doubt— we were in the Quiver Club.

After our eyes adjusted completely to the illumination of the lights we noticed the scented candles situated around the room. I recognized the same type of neo soul music I heard in Rodney's office and Amara's homecoming. We made our way around the ballroom and after about forty-five minutes I decided there was no way possible we were going to find the Thompsons and get a chance to ask them about Amara. There were way too many people in attendance. A few wore masks and were concealing their identity. It seemed as though the other patrons inside felt comfortable enough with one another. By the look of how many hugs and friendly banter during greetings were taking place, the friendships had been established over a period of time, as Rodney explained to us. Lauren was propositioned a few times for her name and number. I couldn't even complain, because she was stunning. We met a few people inside. We gave them fake names. As we made our rounds no one seemed to know Amara. I was beginning to think that another visit might be in order until people inside had become comfortable with us.

After a few hours inside and many drinks to go along with no leads, we ventured our way down the long blue-lit hallway on our way out, following the same man who ushered us in. Our hunt for the Thompsons was a complete bust. Lauren was at her limit and feeling frisky at the same time. I had my arm around her. As we walked past one of the doors that was closed when we walked in, I could see a man in a suit standing just outside the doorway puffing on a cigar with his back toward us. As we go past I could feel him focus on me.

"Well, well, well, look who's decided to come out to play!"

It was Rossi.

Chapter 17

We embraced, then Rossi gave Lauren a hug. The gentleman escorting us back to the car stood by and waited patiently for us, almost as if he was familiar with our long-time friend. Rossi noticed him and greeted Herm, then fixed his eyes on me and Lauren with a grinning, devilish smile. Before I could tell him I could explain our night at the establishment, he was already going in on us.

"Nahhhhhh, not you two guys," he said.

"I don't know what you're talking about, Rossi," I let him know.

Lauren had a smile on her face and told him the same thing as she began to laugh, knowing our friend was about to let us have it.

Rossi had an enormous smile on his face. "I guess it's true . . . you never know. You just never, never know," he said.

"No, you don't know," I told him again. "So, what are you doing here?"

He looked at me. "Can't say." He smiled again. "What are you guys doing here?"

"Can't say," I told him right back.

"Sir, the car is ready to take you back now," Herm let us know.

"That's okay, Herm," Rossi told him. "These are my friends. I'll take care of 'em."

Herm watched us clear away from the establishment. We walked a few steps out the alley to the main
street. Rossi pointed toward a gray BMW 750. Seconds
later, Rossi's mate, Rita, opened the door from the
driver's side. When she noticed Lauren it was like a
high school reunion because they hadn't seen one another in months. Close to a year.

We ended up at Majestic Diner on Ponce De Leon.
Rossi wanted to sit by the window so he could keep
an eye on his machine. Lauren and Rita were dying to
catch up, so they found a seat three tables away and
were already going at it a mile a minute.

I gestured toward Rossi's ride. It was parked right
next to mine. "I see you're saving the money."

"Rita says I look good in it, and you know in this city
it takes money to make money." Rossi reached into his
suit jacket and pulled out an envelope. "And the money
I made tonight is going to help me to continue to do
just that." He opened it up and showed me a wad of
bills, way too much to count. "One hundred large," he
said, folding it up and placing it back into his pocket. "I
owned the tables tonight."

I put two and two together at the night spot we just
left. "That's a hell of an operation they have going," I
mentioned to Rossi.

"Rodney's the truth, man. He's a man of many
ideas." Rossi waited for the waitress to pour our water.
"You and the baby girl enjoy yourselves, tonight? Meet
any *new friends?*"

"Not like we had hoped," I told him. Rossi had his
eyes on me extra tight like never before. I asked him
what the problem was.

"No problem, bro; to each his own is what I always
say."

"Slow down your thoughts. You know how I do
things."

Rossi looked over at the girls. "I always thought I was the wild one in this relationship, man, but you've stolen my crown."

"Believe me, you're still king in that department. I was there looking for someone."

"Oh yeah? Who?"

"Someone to lead us to a killer for a friend of a friend . . . And then there's this two million dollars."

"two million dollars you say?"

Chapter 18

Who would have thought Rossi would be our in? While we broke bread Rossi revealed that he had been a patron of Rodney's poker nights for the past two years. He boasted of big-time connections inside his entire operation. When Rossi heard about the two million he wanted in—but at a price. I couldn't sanction a deal on the prospects of another man's money. But I did have the ability to get everyone in the room to discuss it. Rossi had a private poker game with a few other insiders of Rodney's circle in a few nights. I let Rossi know I would parlay a meeting with him and Tavious Sunday at my shop.

It was storming outside when I arrived at my place of business. It was a few minutes past eleven. Tavious was already there, sitting on the hood of one of the cars left over for the weekend. He didn't speak when I walked in. As I got closer to him I could see he wasn't doing so well.

"Geez, did you even hit the other guy?" I wanted to know.

Tavious had a hell of a bruise under his eye and way too many scars and scrapes to count on his body to go along with his ripped clothing.

I moved in to take a closer look at him. "What the hell happened?"

"Cops . . ."

"Cops?"

"Yeah, the same two police from the other day. They followed me out of the house. I was on my way to get a bite to eat last night. Hit me with the flashing lights, pulled me over—"

I cut him off. "And when you rolled down the window, popped you one, right?"

"How'd you know?"

It had been the same way they treated me a few years ago. I went into the kitchen of my shop to get Tavious some ice. When I returned Rossi and Tavious had already met.

Rossi turned away from Tavious and looked at me. "You see this, West?" Rossi asked.

"Yeah, I see it—Atlanta's finest at their best. And get this, one of the officers following him is the one in the same who dragged us into that vacant house."

"Man, you don't even know what kind of loser scumbags these dudes are," Rossi said to Tavious.

"I think I have an idea now," Tavious admitted. "They dropped me off outside city limits, took all my money, and I had to walk back."

I gave Tavious the ice and he placed it on the side of his head.

"Fuckin' bastards," Rossi let out.

Tavious took the ice from his head then pointed at Rossi. "So, what's this all about, man? I need to go lie down."

I looked at Rossi then back at Tavious. "He has a way in."

Tavious grimaced when he put the ice back on. "What do you mean?"

"When me and Lauren went to the club to check on Rodney's lead, I ran into my old partner in crime—"

Rossi interrupted. "Card game, big night, too—"

I cut Rossi off before he started to embellish the night. "Long story short, we went out to dinner. I told him everything and he is pretty sure he can find out information on who Amara had been hanging out with." Tavious took the ice off. "Well, let's do this."

"I want in," Rossi was very blunt. "I understand there is some money involved and when there is money involved in the streets, I like to involve myself in the game."

"Meaning . . . ?" Tavious wanted to be clear.

"Meaning, I know you want the police off your back; and if I were a betting man, which I am, I would bet you still want your two million dollars you've been waiting on for over twenty years. Now, I've done time, not as much as you, and I can tell you this: when a man gets out, he wants what he wants."

Tavious gave me a look then back at Rossi. "This is your man right, West?"

I slapped Rossi on the back. "In the muthafuckin' flesh," I let him know.

"Cool, what's your price?" Tavious questioned. "I'm sure we can work something out."

Chapter 19

Rossi and Tavious decided on a cool $200,000 if Rossi helped to deliver the money in his hand. When they closed the deal Tavious turned to me and let me know he was now upping my take from one hundred to two hundred Gs along with Rossi to keep things even and to show his appreciation. Rossi was out the door soon after and let us know he would be in touch after he made contact with a few people of interest who were down with TQC.

We were still in the garage and Tavious was still nursing his bumps and bruises. "Man, I have to get out of Grand's place. Those cops already let me know things are only going to get worse and I don't want to worry her."

And I believed every word of what they told him. Especially if they had been trained by Captain Stallings of the APD. He was one of the most ruthless people you'd ever want to meet. They would stop at nothing to make it as uncomfortable for Tavious as possible. He was now on their bad side even though they didn't have any type of evidence that he had killed Amara.

"Any ideas?" I asked.

Tavious sighed. "I've called three places already and everyone wants to know about my rental history, and you know where I've been laying up."

Tavious hadn't caught a break since his release from prison and my empathy for him was growing minute by minute. "So, why don't you take my spot above the garage? Two bedrooms up there, nice living space and kitchen; it's like it was made for you."

"What? You mean like, live there?"

"Yeah, why not?"

"Are you serious?"

"Might as well. It may be the best thing for you because now those freakin' cops can't track you in and out of here. You just walk down to work every morning and back up when you get off."

Tavious saw the light. "Not a bad idea, man. I'll have to tell Grands, but I'm sure she'll understand."

"Of course she would. Hell, she'd be happy for you."

Tavious took the ice from his face. "Done, let's do it. How much is rent?"

"Don't worry, it's on me," I let him know.

"I couldn't just live up there rent free," Tavious said.

"Yes, you can. Just try."

Chapter 20

Later the same night, Rossi came over with Rita after his card game. As usual he was nonstop about his evening card game. I was almost to a point where I wanted to ask him if the gambling bug hadn't attacked his mind to where he was having a problem. After he got it all out of his system he told me he was sure he had an idea to meet the couple Amara was involved with, the Thompsons, but we were going to need the girls to get next to them. He filled me in on his plan after a few drinks; then we took it to the girls while they were in the den watching something on HBO.

"You want us to do what!" Lauren shrieked.

Rita was sitting right down next to her. "Ewww, that's all I'm saying. Ewww; okay, I said it again."

Rossi looked at Rita, knowing she was just acting out because he knew firsthand she has been involved in a lot worse.

Lauren was pretty loud when she asked me, "You want us to go into a club and be interviewed by some couples who like to do the nasty in front of people? Is that what you are asking us to do, West?"

I glanced over at Rossi to be clear and he nodded yes.

Lauren nudged Rita. "I was cool with going to the club with you, West, to take a look-see around. But actually portraying like I want to see somebody get buck-naked and hump and pump is a bit much for this sister here."

Going in, Rossi and I knew that we were not going to get Lauren to do it, not agree to it first, so, like we planned, we turned and looked at Rita.

Rita pushed herself back into her chair. "What? Just because I used to do a few tricks of the trade, you think I would want to see it? Uh-uh. Nope."

"Told you, West. She's lost some of that spice," Rossi said.

"Oh, no, you didn't . . ." Lauren said, giving Rita a pat on the leg to console her.

"You weren't saying that last night," Rita told him.

"Okay," Lauren chimed in. Then she put her hand up as though she was whispering but everyone in the room could hear her. "I had West crying like a baby the other night." They gave one another high fives then began to chuckle.

Rossi looked at me and started shaking his head back and forth.

Rita pointed at Rossi. "And that one standing there . . . I can't even count how many times I've had him curl up in a ball with his thumb in his mouth. Lost my spice, my ass," she said.

I looked at Rossi because our plan to get Rita to agree and Lauren to follow had failed.

"Look, this isn't about us," I let them know.

"Got-damn right, it's about none of us," Rita continued to fuss.

"I heard that," Lauren echoed. "Juicy forever—you know what I mean."

Lauren stood up, took Rita by the hand; and they walked arm and arm into the kitchen.

Chapter 21

There was no way we were going to convince them to do a damn thing in the funk they were in. Rossi was so sure the sex card would play with Rita, but it only pissed her off and we ended up having to take them out to dinner to try to mend things.

Lauren kissed me on the cheek. "Thanks for dinner, boo. Who would have thought you would have brought us down to Ruth's Chris and get me that one hundred and fifty dollar steak. It was so . . . good." Then she gave me three more kisses after that.

"No problem," I let Lauren know. "Anything for you, babe."

We looked over at Rossi while Rita was finishing her fourth glass of wine.

"Aren't you going to thank me?" Rossi wanted to know.

She wiped her mouth with her napkin. "Thank you," she said. "So, when exactly do you need us to be at the W, hon?"

Rossi looked at me and back at Rita. "I never told you the interviews were at the W."

"I know, but I heard you telling West where it was and I had to let Lauren know before we made you take us to dinner."

Chapter 22

The next week of work was as ordinary as they come. There were no pressing issues at the shop that threatened to make my blood pressure sky rocket. And the guys in the shop were getting them fixed just as fast as they were coming in. Tavious hadn't had any more run-ins with the cops. More than likely because they weren't able to grab him off the street since he now was going straight from the shop to the apartment upstairs.

It was Friday night and the time had come for the ladies to shine in their interviews at the club. Rossi came by and picked us up a little past seven. We made it to the W close to eight o'clock. Yummy is all I could say. My baby Lauren was looking amazing. She was wearing a black dress that brought out her stunning curves on her body. Rita was looking scrumptious as well. She had on a red dress with her twins sitting high and tight for all to see. The plan was for the ladies to go in one at a time and try to locate the Thompsons, who were friendly with Amara, and we would sit in the car and wait for their return. As we sat in the car the only thing exciting was Rossi's new haircut.

"I was told that at least forty couples RSVPed," Rossi let me know.

"Cool, and all we need is one," I said.

For the umpteenth time Rossi smoothed his hand over his now-bald head.

I turned to him. "So, what's up with this haircut?"

"Oh, this?"

"Yeah, that."

"Rita wanted me to get it. Said I would look good."

"You sure are blaming a lot of shit on your girl these days. First this piece-of-shit car, now your head. I'm beginning to wonder about you."

"Why?"

"Just saying, man, you got a perfect head full of hair and you cut it off?"

"I already told you. She likes it. It's a change."

We waited some more and watched a few couples go into the W Hotel hand in hand wondering which ones were going inside to be a part of the interview process.

Rossi plopped a mint in his mouth. "So, how sure are you that there is even two million dollars?"

"I can tell you I've never seen it because it wasn't there when we went to the house. But I did see the dead body and the space where it could have been hidden. But I wouldn't have a reason to doubt Tavious or I wouldn't be here. He did twenty, man—a twenty-year bid for drug trafficking. Mrs. Bullock told me that much."

Rossi was a stickler for knowing the facts. When I first met him he would test me by asking me a question, then wait for some time to elapse, then ask the same question again to see if he got the same answer.

We ended up having to line the pockets of the valet with fifty dollars to allow us to stay sitting parked in our car at the front of the hotel. Rossi walked down Lenox to a hamburger joint and brought us back burgers and large drinks. In the meantime, I called Tavious to see if he was finished setting up the apartment. I also let him know we were waiting for the girls to come out.

Lauren and Rita had been inside close to three hours and we figured they hadn't run into the Thompsons yet or they would have come out right after.

"What do you think this couple is like?" Rossi wanted to know. "You really have to be comfortable with one another to invite someone in your bed, man."

I paused for a while because when I met Rita I remember her and Rossi going at it a mile a minute right in front of my face. It took everything I had not to make light of Rossi and remind him but I held it for another time. "Yeah, you really have to be in another zone, man."

Finally, at a little past twelve that night, I spot Lauren coming out. She sees us and comes over to the car. She sat down inside and exhaled. "Whew, never in my life." We both had our eyes on her. "West, I am telling you," she said.

"What are you telling us?" Rossi wanted to know.

Lauren looked at him odd. "Did you get a haircut while I was up in there?"

Rossi looked over at me. "No, no, I didn't, Lauren. Can you just tell us what happened? Where's Rita?"

"I don't know where she is. I didn't even see her. Can you believe they had us meet these couples by their last names? I mean, I was freaking looking for the Thompsons and I had to wait that entire time to finally meet them."

Rossi pushed. "You met them? What did they say? Did you get a contact number or something?"

"No." Lauren flipped off her shoes then saw the wrappers from the burgers we had and let us know she wanted one too.

Rossi kept on. "No number? Why not?"

"'Cause I didn't like the way he was looking at me," Lauren said.

I am pretty sure we both said, "What?" at the same time.

Lauren started to fidget around. "He was looking at me all freaky and shit, baby . . . I mean how many times does he have to lick his lips when talking? I know they wanted someone to watch them, but I think they were on some real freaky shit. I can't exactly put my finger on it but they were some kind of freaky."

Rossi slid down in his seat and grabbed the steering wheel. "Fuck me."

"That's right, Mr. Rossi, fuck you," Lauren told hm.

I tried to calm things down because Lauren and Rossi still would go at each other's throats for any reason, anytime, not out of hatred but because it is what they enjoyed about one another. They went on and on for a few minutes over my objection and then finally Rita came strutting out like she was reliving her prior life before Rossi.

As soon as she sat down Rossi started in on her. "How'd everything go?"

"Wow . . ." Rita said. Then she sat back, exhausted, in the back seat. "Wow . . ." she repeated.

Lauren was still rubbing her feet. "Girl, are you okay?" Lauren wanted to know.

"Yes . . . Wow . . . Wow," Rita purred.

"Rita, you better tell me something besides wow, or I'm going up in that place and kicking somebody's ass," Rossi said. "I just know you didn't—"

Rita cut him off. "Hush it up right there, Mr. Man, I'm okay . . ."

Lauren looked at Rossi. "I don't know, maybe you did . . ."

"No, it's just the atmosphere in there. Who would have thought I sold my pussy for two years and I could have joined this club and probably gotten paid to watch; this world is fucked . . . up." Then she started in with her deep, bellowing laughter.

"Whatever, whatever; did you meet the Thompsons?" I asked her.

"Yes, I met them," she said.

"I did too," Lauren added.

All of a sudden Rita looked out the front window from the back seat and pointed at them. "There they are . . . right there."

We all see a rather tall white man with a black woman under his arm wearing a tight dress.

"There they are, the Thompsons," Rita said.

Then almost immediately Lauren saw another couple exit the W walking in the opposite direction; then she began to point. "No, no, those two right there are the Thompsons," she let us know.

Chapter 23

Turns out that both couples were named Thompson and we had to act quickly because it seemed as though our entire night could have been for naught. When Rita told us that she exchanged Facebook accounts with *her* Thompsons we decided to keep an eye on the other pair, and watched as they walked down Lenox and into a swanky-looking bar.

After about twenty minutes of back and forth, Lauren gave in and decided that she would go in and "accidently" run into the Thompsons again. She wasn't happy about it. We waited long enough for her to have a drink with them. Rossi waited inside across the bar, keeping a close eye on her. When she returned and filled us in on their conversation we were 100 percent sure they were not the Thompsons on our radar. Their kink was flirting with women and only allowing men to join them in the bedroom.

I had always been amazed at how the Internet and social media applications brought people together. But more so by how quickly Rita was able to connect and become very intimate with her new friends the Thompsons. We confirmed that their names were Charles and Gale and they lived in Cobb County in a nice and quiet private spread. Charles was a surgeon and Gale had a high-profile position with an Atlanta law firm.

When Rita reached out to them they accepted her friend request. The first day they shared fifteen messages and during the night spent close to three hours just chatting on instant messenger. Charles and Gale had become more than ready to meet with Rita in real time but she continued on her objective to get any information she could muster on Amara without mentioning her name. But no matter how she tried they would not give any information about anyone who they could have been intimate with. Charles began to talk about his interns on his job and how he had them follow him on Twitter to follow his daily activities. He sent Rita an invite to follow him and once again the Internet had turned out to be our friend because we found out he loved to eat lunch at the same place and time every day.

I called Tavious and asked him if he wanted to do lunch.

I'd never imagined a hospital cafeteria to be so crowded and right away I thanked the man upstairs for never really having to know. We knew the good doctor came into eat at preciously one-fifteen because he tweeted it. He sat right next to a wall facing a flower bed with the white marble birdbath just like he told everyone in cyber space that he would. Tavious and I were sitting and waiting when he arrived and we decided to get a bite to eat, too.

"I can't fuckin' believe people will put their every move on a computer screen so anyone can follow what they're doing," Tavious mentioned. "Shit is as bad as prison, if you ask me."

"Well, I know at least one activity he's not telling anyone about."

Tavious grabbed his drink and shook his head. "I don't get it, West; technology has taken over the world in twenty years, man. GPS, texting, computers, cell phones, books in a machine. Amara told me it was crazy out here but where in the fuck am I? Look around . . . more people in this café looking down at their fuckin' machines than talking to one another."

I'm sure life and everyday living had to be a change for Tavious. Probably in his eyes it was like he was stepping into a world from which he was far removed. I could sometimes see his frustrations with some of the cars we'd get in the shop and the computers that told us how to do our job, or even the computers that make the cars actually run.

We waited in the lunchroom at least twenty minutes before we went over. Charles was a few minutes into the front page of the *AJC*. We finally walked over and I spoke first.

"Dr. Thompson?"

He looked up from his paper and quickly scanned me and then Tavious with his eyes before he ran his hand through his dark hair and answered. "Yes." He looked to be over six feet and in pretty good shape, maybe a runner or boxer type.

"My name is West, do you mind if we have a bit of your time?"

He was clearly confused. "But I—"

"It's about Amara," Tavious let him know; then he sat down without an invite.

There was a quiet pause and the good doctor looked around the cafeteria. "I . . . I didn't get your name," he said.

"My name is Tavious Bell. A friend of Amara's."

The doctor softened. "Tavious . . . ? Yes, yes . . . I've heard all about you."

Tavious inched up closer to hear what the doctor had to say, and the doctor's face told me he could feel his anxiety.

"Just a figure of speech. But yes, I've heard Amara say your name several times . . . if you know what I mean." Then he smiled.

"Okay, since we got that all out the way, can you tell us what happened to her?

The doctor paused. "Can you tell me how you found me?"

"Internet," I let him know.

"That got-damn Twitter no doubt. I teach a class at Georgia Tech and it's a part of the territory. Got-damn technology, whole world can find out what you're doing. Fuckin' gadgets—we've become too spoiled. Spoiled to no end." He pointed to his paper. "Look here: yesterday two teenage girls killed their mother. For what? I bet they were given everything they ever wanted in life and never told no. Or worse yet they're a fuckin' result of that crack epidemic. I see it all the time, mothers who smoked that shit—their kids have turned out to be fuckin' devils I tell you . . . devils."

"Yeah, it's a bad situation, but you're clear why we are here, right?"

The doctor shook his head no but said yes.

"Amara. We need to find out who killed her and if she had any other contacts in the club who got you guys together," I said.

"My, you guys know my life story or something?"

"It would probably take us a few days but we could get it," I let him know.

"Wouldn't even have to ask Gale," Tavious boasted.

The doctor put his paper down. "Look, I don't know what to tell you. I told the police everything I know."

I wanted to know about the police and asked him about it.

"Two cops came to see me. That's how I found out she had died. They found my card with my number in her bedroom and wanted to know our relationship. And they asked if I knew you." He pointed at Tavious.

"What did these officers look like?"

"Um, I don't know. One white, the other black," he said.

"What did you tell them?" Tavious asked.

"I gave Amara all the respect she deserves. The only thing I told them was that she came to my office for a consultation."

I asked him what type of consultation.

"I told them it was confidential and couldn't divulge it to them. But she was fine. I just didn't want to scar her memory in any way; plus, it's none of their damn business what people do in their private lives."

"Including yours," I mentioned.

He pointed at me. "Exactly."

"She ever mention if anyone was after her? Was she scared of anything?"

"Amara didn't have an ounce of fear in her body. Like I said, all she talked about was waiting until you got home and how her life would change. To me, she was head over heels with you and wanted you, man."

Tavious had a look on his face that if he heard that again he would explode.

"How long did you know her?" I asked him.

"A couple of years."

We sat and talked until his next scheduled surgery. When we left the only things we knew were that the detectives had paid him a visit and Amara was not heavy into their wild and kinky lifestyle while caring for Tavious a great deal all along. On the way out of the hospital the first thing Tavious said was concerning the story in the paper the doctor spoke of. He wanted me to know that he never sold crack and these bad kids running the streets are not a result of what he did in his past.

Chapter 24

We were in the car and back to square one. No leads, no clues. Tavious seemed very uncomfortable to me and I asked him if he was okay.

He was looking out the window. Didn't even look back at me when he spoke. "I just got out of prison, man. I have the damn police asking questions about me. This is bullshit, West. We need to find out who else was involved with Amara. She had to have someone in her life closer to her than these freakin' fools we've met so far. Just doesn't make sense."

I couldn't agree with him more. Amara lived alone and from what I could tell had deeper feelings for Tavious than he ever knew and enjoyed sex on some type of abstinence level. I'd always had the philosophy "to each his own" and my intuition was telling me that she was saving herself for Tavious but didn't want to keep her needs unmet to a certain point. I was all out of ideas on which direction we should go to keep Tavious from being harassed by the police or even being charged, because I knew if the police were coming up goose eggs like we were. They were going to make a case against Tavious and do whatever they could to make it stick.

Tavious agreed to have dinner with us at my place. Rita and Rossi called to let us know they were on their way, and when we walked in everyone was in the kitchen, surrounding the island, looking at Rita's laptop.

"Look at this," Rita said, pointing to the computer screen. "Amara has a Facebook page and someone is online at this very moment."

Tavious moved in to get a closer look. "Let me see that."

"Whoever has her account has been online for the past two hours," Rossi said.

Lauren said, "Either she's online in heaven—or begging for help in hell."

"This could be our chance to find out what's goin' on," Tavious said.

"I could try inviting whoever this is to be a friend," Rita suggested.

"But that might scare them off," Lauren said.

"We just can't sit here and not do anything, because you never know when they'll be online again."

There was pause.

"Try to talk to them," Tavious said.

"What?" Rita said.

"Everyone we have met so far has at least heard of me." Tavious became excited. "Hurry, say hello to them and tell them it's Tavious. Tavious Bell."

Rita looked around.

"Go ahead, do it. Whoever that is has my life in their hands."

Rita maneuvered around everyone and in no time did exactly what Tavious asked.

Hey, Amara. It's Tavious. Tavious Bell.

Then there was a return message: Tavious. Meet me at Screen on the Green. Don't sit. Stand.

Everyone read the message planted across the computer screen, and it was followed by silence, then a jolt of energy. We were back in the game. Tavious was hyped with his aggressiveness to give his name in cyberspace; but slightly deflated after he questioned what the Screen on the Green was and Lauren let him know there were thousands of people at the event at any given time, and a place where someone could see you without you even knowing.

"It's a really big event. People watching a movie out on the lawn, the place is very crowded," Lauren let Tavious know.

Rossi added, "Public meet and greets always diffuse problems; somebody is playing it safe."

"You think we are talking to Amara's killer? If we are, we need to play it safe for damn sure," Tavious promised.

"Can't tell," Rita said. "But it's obvious whoever this is knows something."

It was time to go sit down in the family room and get in defensive mode. I knew that whoever it was must be living in Atlanta, and if Tavious did make contact with the person we were going to have to follow them and find out where they lived without them knowing.

It took us a few hours to figure out a plan. Tavious would be alone and I would sit closely by with Lauren on a blanket watching his every move. Rita and Rossi were going to be close on the street in the car and we would call one another every ten minutes on the cell. When Tavious made contact I would call Rossi and Rita so they could follow whoever Tavious met to their home so we would have a definite contact on them.

Chapter 25

Thursday couldn't have come quick enough. The plan was to put in a good day's work at the shop, then go over to the Screen on the Green. We didn't know who we were dealing with so we had to be extra careful. The only thing we knew about the person who asked to meet Tavious was that they were using a dead woman's Facebook account. This could have been our break as to who killed Amara and stole the two million. Of course this was one of the times that I was happy that I took the time to go get my permit to carry. The decision was made early on that we were not going to do anything by force. That was not even in the cards. We just wanted to get contact and an address, and find the money before turning the killer over to the police, so that Tavious could stay a free man.

When we arrived we positioned ourselves in the back of the seating arrangements so that Tavious could stand and walk around the setup in the park. The whole night was strange because we were waiting for someone we didn't know, and we didn't know when they would show up. After an hour after the movie started it became dark. When Tavious walked back in our direction he gave me a look of confusion. Rossi and Rita were on the phone as scheduled every ten to fifteen minutes wondering what was happening as well. Lauren knew the movie playing had only thirty or so minutes left. When the movie ended there was no one there to meet Tavious.

We packed it up and went back to my place.

"What the hell was that, man?" Tavious said as I poured him a drink.

"Somebody is messing with you," Rossi said.

"But who?' Lauren questioned.

"I don't know, but whoever it is just pissed me off," I told them.

"You?" Tavious said. "I wanted to stop every person who looked at me and ask them their name."

"Uh-ooooh . . ." we heard Rita sing.

Lauren walked over to her to find out what was going on.

"It's our friend on Facebook again," Rita told her.

We all gathered around and read the screen.

You look good in red. J Meet me at the Waffle House in Hapeville in thirty minutes.

Rita didn't wait for anyone to tell her what to type this time. She asked the person on the other end who they were, but didn't get an answer. Rossi knew Hapeville all too well. Years ago before I met him, it was the exact spot where he found himself in a heap of trouble working with the police in a drug sting operation. It was getting a bit too late so we asked our ladies to stay behind in case there was trouble. Rita said she would monitor the computer and Lauren would wait by the phone to hear back from me.

I had a reason not to like Rossi's German piece-of-shit BMW and I told him so. It wasn't made in America. And it helped put lots of skilled workers in the street. Matter of fact, a Ford plant in Hapeville that we were about to pass had been shut down just years before. But I had to give the Beemer props. That freaking car was a beast on the road and Rossi boasted about it the entire way. We were at our location in fifteen minutes, sitting outside in the parking lot, looking into the Waffle House. Rossi was going to stay behind the wheel of the car, keep it running just in case we would need a quick getaway. I went inside with Tavious with my Black Widow revolver in my pants pocket.

When we walked inside there was no mistaking by the aroma that the grill was hot and at the ready. We tried to leave space between us as we walked in but it was almost impossible. The establishment was very small and we scanned the restaurant as best as we could. There was a couple sitting on the right-hand side next to a window. Both had coffee.

Another couple on the opposite side of them was giving their order to the waitress. A woman was sitting at the counter with her back toward us. And a white man was all the way to the back of the diner with a glass of water sitting in front of him, staring at us. He had a scruffy beard. He was wearing a tan jacket. I noticed his hands were under the table. For some reason he kept his eyes on us. We agreed with our eyes that he was the person we were there to see. I walked behind Tavious with my hand close to my pocket where Ms. Widow sat. When we were just a few steps from the man the woman sitting at the barstool with her back to us turned around and grabbed Tavious by his arm.

"Hey, son," she said.

Chapter 26

Seconds later the entire Waffle House parking lot was filled with police cars. Swirling emergency lights were illuminating and officers vaulted out of their cars. It happened quickly but I noticed a man in blue yank Rossi out of his car as I looked out the large restaurant window. The police were wild and reckless as though they were having a bad-ass night. They stormed inside. In seconds I was in handcuffs along with Tavious. We were headed to the police station. It was so close to the restaurant that they could have walked us there instead of throwing us in the back seats of their cruisers.

We were all taken to different rooms. They took the cuffs off me. Made me sit down in a hot cinderblock room painted in gray. I could faintly hear the officers say Rossi's name before they shut my door. A few seconds later I hear Rossi tell them to all kiss his ass as they walk past my room. I was more pissed than anything because when I told a young officer, after he asked if I had anything in my pockets, that I had a pistol, he pushed my head down on a Waffle House table. He was trying to receive points from fellow officers who kept calling him rookie.

After about thirty minutes of sitting alone in the rank room that someone had relieved themselves in, Williams, the black officer who came into my office with no sense, walked in. He passed by my chair and faced a concrete wall. His boy Gus was close behind.

"What's wrong, your boyfriend, Gus, on his cycle?" I asked him.

He turned around, exhaled, then put his index finger over his lips.

I looked at Gus. "I was right then?"

Williams walked over to the table. He slammed his hand on top of it and told me to shut the fuck up.

I asked him, "*Law & Order* right?"

"Do you mind telling me what the fuck you are doing in Waffle House with a loaded pistol?"

I told him, "Permit to carry, next question."

"Well, I seem to remember that you and your boy next door got into a little trouble in this part of town a few years ago. And here you are back again; any coincidence as to the reason why?"

I shook my head no.

"Look here, damn it. I am not here to play games with you. I have a murder on my hands. A murder of a woman. Your ex-con hack of a mechanic was very friendly with her. Now, do you care to tell me what the fuck is going on? Why are you and Rossi hanging out with this asshole dope dealer?"

I made sure he was looking me in the eyes before I answered. "We're his big brothers," I told him. "Now, arrest me for something or I'm walking out."

Williams exhaled. I took it as he was defeated and I stood on my feet. There was nothing they had on me and they knew it. And I knew my rights and wanted to get out that room reeking of piss and alcohol mix because it was beginning to make me sick.

"Who has my heat?" I wanted to know.

Williams pointed toward the outside and I left the room, keeping an eye on Gus. I had to walk down a hallway to get to the front desk. When I got there a woman police officer was sitting behind a bulletproof window. She was wearing glasses and reading *O Magazine*. I gave her my name and asked for my weapon back. She asked me to produce my ID. I told her I couldn't because that was taken from me, too. The officer was forced to get off her ass because no one would answer her on the radio to return my belongings. I turned around when the door from the outside of the police station was opened. It was the woman who called Tavious "son."

She looked at me when she stepped inside. I quickly scanned her without saying a word to see if she had any resemblance to Tavious. Early forties, brown skin, short haircut, five six with light brown eyes. A purse was draped over her shoulder.

"He looks like his father," she said.

"Hi, I'm West," I let her know. "Friend of Tavious's."

"Joyce. I'm Joyce Bullock. I'm Tavious's mother."

I kind of smile at her and remember vaguely Tavious telling me he hadn't heard nor seen his mother in over twenty years. For no other reason I thought about him wondering how it felt to see her for that brief moment before he was arrested.

"Is he still in there? Why'd they take him?"

"I don't know," I told her.

We both look down the hall when we hear yelling.

"Fuck you!"

It was Rossi and his voice was getting closer and closer to us.

"And there better not be a scratch on my got-damn car, you sons of bitches. You can't just snatch someone out the car for no damn reason. Got-damn assholes!"

Now standing next to me, Rossi smoothed out his clothes. He tried his best to regain his composure.

"Okay?" I asked him.

"Yeah," he said. He straightened out his shirt some more. "They are about to bring it out of me, man. Let's get out of here," he said.

"Can't, waiting on my belongings," I told him.

Rossi nodded at Joyce as she stood behind us, then turned back around.

"She's Tavious's mother," I told him.

Rossi looked back at her and acknowledged her again. "West, what's going on, man? Where is he anyway?"

Joyce was getting impatient. "They think he killed Amara don't they?" she said.

I looked around to make sure no one heard her. Rossi opened the entrance door to the police station and I put my arm around Joyce. We walked her out into the parking lot.

"Look, I don't think you should be talking about that right now," I let her know.

"I'm going to go get my car and come back and wait for you," Rossi let us know.

I asked Joyce if she would walk with Rossi to pick up his car because it wasn't safe talking in front of the police station. She agreed. When I got back into the police station it took the lady officer another thirty minutes before she came out with my things. I was sure they were trying to mess with me, seeing as I was the only person waiting in the lobby.

Finally, she brought them out. As soon as I finished making sure everything was in my wallet, and my pistol was, in fact, mine with no missing rounds, I met up with Rossi and Joyce, who were out in the car.

Chapter 27

When I got my things back and turned on my phone I could see that Lauren had called way more than a few times. I called the ladies to let them know we were okay. Joyce was now in the back seat of Rossi's car. She was drinking a coffee from Waffle House. It didn't seem to be helping her cope that her son who she hadn't seen in twenty years was still in jail.

"I had a feeling they were going to come after him for this," she said. "I tried to wait around for him at her house because she told me he was on his way, but I got scared. I didn't want anybody to see me."

"You were at Amara's house?" I asked.

She nodded her head yes.

"Why'd you go there?" Rossi asked.

"We were going to surprise Tavious. I knew Amara some when the two would hang out and do their thing. I kept in contact with her the entire time he was in prison without him knowing. She was my funnel to my son. Every time they would talk she would let me know how he was doing. I wasn't so sure about it, but she talked me into coming to see him first thing when he got out and I agreed. When I went over to see her, the front door was open. When I walked in, there she was, just above the stairs, dead."

"Did you see anyone coming or going?"

"Not a soul. I knocked on the door; it was slightly open. I went in when she didn't answer; then I saw her on the floor in her blood." There was a pause. Joyce, no doubt, was reflecting. I was watching her in the rear-view mirror.

Rossi turned around. "Did you take anything?"

"Like what?" Joyce answered quickly.

"Like anything?" Rossi repeated.

"Amara had a suitcase next to the door. When I left I picked it up and took it with me."

"Suitcase?"

"Yes, a brown suitcase. She told me that she and Tavious were going to go on a vacation."

"What was in the suitcase?" I wanted to know.

"Just some clothes and her laptop."

Rossi turned around again. "That's it?"

"That's it," she responded.

"So, that's how you got on her Facebook page?"

"Yes. I turned on her computer and it automatically came up. I didn't have to put in a password or any-thing—the computer must have been in sleep mode or something. I thought about closing down her page but I thought I would just let it be; then I got a message from Tavious."

"Why didn't you meet him at the park," I asked her.

"Scared . . . I don't know. It's been twenty years so I didn't go through with it when I saw his face. I know he's staying with my mother but I haven't seen her either."

We sat and chatted with Joyce a few more minutes. She was not in the chatting mood. She wanted to go inside the police station and find out what she could about her son. She didn't trust the police any more than I did. Joyce kept rambling that they were proba-bly inside trying to get him to confess to killing Amara. Rossi pulled into the parking lot. I got out of the front seat and opened the door for her. As she made her way out of the car a black sedan pulled up next to us. The back window rolled down.

"Joyce?" Mrs. Bullock questioned.

"Mama?" Joyce said back. "They've got Tavious again."

Chapter 28

Soon after that, Rossi and I were standing alone in the well-lit police parking lot. We were sure there were cameras and cops looking out at us. At this point there was no hiding from the police that we were connected to Tavious on a more personal level than employment. The night was turning out to give us a little insight into Tavious and his personal life. Mrs. Bullock and Joyce stood outside for at least twenty minutes talking then hugging before they ended up walking inside the police station hand in hand.

About ten minutes after they went inside, Mrs. Bullock, Joyce, and Tavious were walking out the door. Mrs. Bullock seemed as stern as I've seen her in years. Tavious was straightening his collar on his jacket and getting himself back together while looking outward at us standing in front of Rossi's car. Everyone turned to a black Ford F-150 that inched onto the lot. The driver began to faintly blow its horn more than a few times. The truck stopped right in front of Rossi's BMW. The driver door opened. There was a gigantic German shepherd inside. The dog was not happy that it was being left alone. It was barking out of its mind. The beast kept his eyes on the man now outside the truck. It pawed and growled with some crazy distain. Rossi grabbed the handle of his own car, ready to jump his ass inside.

The black man was now in front of his truck. He was average height with a short haircut. He initiated a hand signal in the direction of the window of his truck and the dog immediately stopped his nonsense like it was remote activated.

Rossi whispered, "You see this shit?"

"Joyce? Joyce, you okay?" This guy repeated himself at least three times. He looked over at me then Rossi. He seemed a bit hesitant when he joined up with Joyce, who was standing with Tavious and her mother.

Joyce introduced them. "Ma, Tavious, this is my husband, Ely," she let them know.

"You're married?" Mrs. Bullock asked.

"Almost a month now," Joyce let her know.

Her husband reached out and shook Mrs. Bullock's hand while Tavious gave him a glancing over and just acknowledged him by barely moving his chin upward an inch. After Ely asked Joyce if she was okay again, Mrs. Bullock suggested to Tavious that he go home with her. He declined. She walked over to me.

"West, you of all people know my reach in these parts. I got a call and I'm here. At the moment I don't know what's going on. But I'll trust you will fill me in after I get some rest," Mrs. Bullock said.

Chapter 29

I still had business to attend to in my shop. With everything going on it made it that much more difficult to keep up with the normal daily grind. But I had to admit—the intrigue of what was unfolding around Tavious had my juices flowing a bit more than what my shop had to offer. I was chasing something, but I didn't know where it existed nor what was causing the problem, and I enjoyed it all. I realized it was almost like when I started repairing cars. I would get a thrill of trying to figure out what was going on with a distressed ride, opposed to later in life when I could almost diagnose what was wrong with a car just by someone telling me the problem they were having with it.

Lauren didn't hesitate to step up and help out more than usual to take the load off me. Her presence in the shop allowed me to go see Mrs. Bullock when she called during the midday wanting to see me.

I hadn't been over to see Mrs. Bullock at her estate in quite some time. She had a little more help around the place than I could remember. I noticed a cook, an assistant back in her office, and a man outside putting in new light bulbs in fixtures. She walked in her study and as always with a smile.

"Thanks for coming, West."

I let her know it wasn't a problem at all.

She sat down across from me in a French-style brown leather chair. "You know why I asked you over?"

I nodded my head in agreement.

"So, I'll just get right to it. It hurts to ask this. And I know deep in my heart what kind of boy—well, man—Tavious was raised to be. But I need to know if you think he killed this young woman."

Now it was official. Mrs. Bullock has found out that Tavious was being investigated. I knew deep down inside that she would find out sooner or later. As I sat in front of her I could have kicked myself for not being the one to tell her about what was going on. I didn't want to add any stress to her life so I decided not to. I hoped that she wouldn't hold it against me and by the type of person she was I didn't think she would. From that moment on, I decided that all info I had on Tavious and what was going on with him I was going to give to Mrs. Bullock straight with no chaser, even though I could see the worry all over her face.

"Mrs. Bullock, there is no doubt in my mind that Tavious didn't kill her."

She exhaled. "I never thought he did, but hearing it from you puts my heart at ease," she confided.

"But I do think the police, just because they have an open murder case and no other leads, are trying to pin the murder on Tavious. He needs to find out who did kill his friend so that doesn't happen."

"Well, I've seen them send men to prison with much less evidence than what they have on my grandson. Ex-cons are always the first choice whenever they can be connected to a crime." She thinks. "You know, West . . . I'd have never imagined Tavious would have to live his life this way, even though his mother wasn't there for him like I was raised to be there for my children. You see, she was always in and out of his life . . . searching for what was best for herself, very selfish. His grandfather and I tried to make sure he had the best of everything,

which probably made his mother believe she didn't
have to do much. She had the leeway to not be as good
a mother as she could have been. We could give him the
best schools, best of care, but everything we put into
him never seemed to come out. I think it was because
he wanted his mother in his life; and to make matters
worse, the poor boy never knew his father. No one did.
But through all that madness I can see, even though he
has been locked away in that godforsaken place, he still
has some good left in him and a murderer he's not."

I agreed with Mrs. Bullock. To me Tavious was the
type of person who didn't like confrontation. He was
someone who just wanted to do his time, whether it be
behind prison walls or free as a bird.

Mrs. Bullock looked at me sternly. "Do I know everything that's going on here? It seems on the surface that
something else is brewing."

There was no way I could look Mrs. Bullock in the
face and lie to her. I told her that weeks ago Tavious
asked me to go over Amara's house with him to look
for his two million, and when we arrived she was dead.
It wasn't comfortable filling her in on all the details. I
explained to her that we had information on some of
the places Amara would hang out, but after checking
them all out, there wasn't a soul who didn't seem to like
Amara or who we thought would harm her.

Mrs. Bullock looked down at her tea in thought while
she moved her head back and forth, trying to decide
what to say next. No doubt she was deep in thought.

"Looks like you have yourself another case, West."
She kind of smiled at me.

"Excuse me?"

"Who would have thought we would be right back
here again?" she said with a coy smile planted on her
face.

I was fully aware of what Mrs. Bullock's smile was all about. She wanted me in 100 percent to help her grandson. It all brought back memories when Rossi and I helped her put those ruthless bastards in jail who worked for the Atlanta Police Department. She thought I had a knack for solving cases and never let me forget it.

There was no uncertainty that I enjoyed solving problems. Maybe deep down inside, way deep, my motivation came from that smooth television character in the late eighties played by Avery Brooks in *A Man They Call Hawk*. He was the only black man I ever saw who was allowed to walk around strapped with that long-ass pistol and wave it around in everybody's face. The aura of it all got to a point where I never missed an episode. But Tavious and his predicament were real. I could only pray that I could help him, because if I didn't I think it would possibly kill Mrs. Bullock to see him go off to prison again.

Chapter 30

On every Sunday since he had been out of the pen Tavious made sure that he would have breakfast with Mrs. Bullock. It was one of the few family traditions he still remembered and missed dearly when he was locked up. His grandmother had a cook but never let her touch the sacred meal on Sunday morning since he had been released. Mrs. Shirley Bullock thought it was too precious of a day. Besides, Tavious loved her grits, fish, and eggs even when he was a little boy.

The menu for the morning feast was already planned and prepared: waffles, omelets, some biscuits, and a gang of fresh fruit including Tavious's favorite California seedless grapes.

"Is everything the way you like it, Tavious?"

"Grands, you still got it," Tavious let her know.

He noticed his grandmother smile. She was even proud.

Tavious stood up and gave his grandmother his plate for this third round. "How do you do it? It's just how I remembered."

"It's all love, baby. When you put love into it, your love is bound to come out in the taste and it makes people feel good," she said. "Big problem with these women today, too," she said.

Tavious took the plate after it was nice and full. "What's that?"

"Tavious, they can't cook, baby," she said. "Over the past twenty or so years, these young ladies haven't been taught the difference between a pot and a pan." That in fact was a huge topic of discussion with Mrs. Bullock and her friends at the senior center in downtown Atlanta.

She was adamant about women and their craft of cooking. She believed that spending time in the kitchen preparing a meal was a way to a man's heart. She had evidence because she'd kept her husband for over fifty years happy as can be every night.

Tavious chuckled as he stuffed another homemade butter biscuit in his mouth then reached for his coffee mug. Mrs. Bullock placed a newspaper down on the table next to him. He looked down and started to read the headline staring him in the face: ALL ALONE AND MURDERED.

"Looks like a reporter has taken interest into what happened with your friend," his grandmother said.

She had read the article twice hours before passing it to Tavious. Ever since her husband played such an important role in Atlanta city politics it had become her ritual to scour the paper to find out what was happening in the city. She had read many articles from this particular reporter, Saadia Eussit. She was a clever, seasoned reporter who had the knack for concentrating on the facts of situations and only offering opinions and commentary in her biweekly column.

Tavious had not taken his eyes from the paper since seeing the headline. He did sip on his coffee a few times as he read without showing any reaction to what it said. When he finished he exhaled, then held out his coffee mug and his grandmother was already there ready to give him a refill.

"So, it's in the paper now," he mentions.

"Yes, a lady murdered for no apparent reason is the type of stories reporters in this town salivate for."

"She doesn't seem to have much," he said. "Seems to know as much as everybody else."

"She'll find out more; she always does," his grandma assured him. "The brass down at the *AJC* gives her full reign to do pretty much what she wants. She's not an unethical woman by any stretch but she does get her stories at all cost. Thank God she didn't use your name in the paper. But when she finds out you've been questioned, there will be no way to keep you out of it when people finally get interested and want to know what's going on."

Tavious looked at the paper and slid it to the other side of the table. There was a moment of silence.

"I think you should go see her." Mrs. Bullock's words were as blunt as the day she told him she believed he could ride his bike and the only thing he had to do was to actually do it.

"You want me to go see the woman who could possibly tell the whole city I am a killer?"

"That's exactly the reason to go see her. Give her your side of the story before any innuendos or any false allegations are made by the police. Times have changed over the years, Tavious. You have to use the media as an advantage because if you ever—God forbid—ever have to go to trial, public opinion will play a part of the outcome."

Tavious was silent and all he wanted at the time was more coffee.

Chapter 31

Tavious remained in the kitchen after his conversation with his Grands. He wanted to relax and take in his grandmother's thoughts while enjoying the light breeze wafting and bouncing through the windows. Gospel music— inspirational to some—was blaring throughout the house. "No Weapon Formed Against Me Shall Prosper." Tavious was at ease of sorts despite the revealing news article about Amara's death written by this Saadia Eussit.

Unannounced or planned his mother Joyce came into the kitchen. Seeing her was not on his agenda. Seeing her at the Waffle House and outside in the parking lot was cool enough. His plan today was to sit back, focus, and think of an idea to get his two million, then live comfortably without her in his life at all. That's it.

"It sure is good to see you, baby," she said.

Her voice was agitating. Tavious didn't want to do this now. His group therapy sessions in prison with detailed ways to deal with negative distractions were going to help him with this stress. He turned them on. His old, bearded counselor's voice appeared in his head. It reminded him to control himself. He remembered how to do just that. *Breathe.* It was going to be difficult though. He had years of built-up electrons bubbling inside his body. They were close to spilling over. He still couldn't believe she didn't come and see her own son in prison.

Tavious suppressed everything running through his mind with silence. *Not a word. Steady, deep breaths.*

"You barely said a word to me the other night," his mother pushes.

The second sound of her voice is even more irritating. It rattled his brain more than her words. He remained silent but pushed and tapped his foot under the table akin to stomping down on a kick drum pedal in a concert for a rapper where it needed to be loud as can be.

"Tavious, I know you're upset with me. And you have every right to be, but we have to talk sometime," she pressed.

Tavious doesn't respond. He was still working on his breathing technique and still recoiling with his leg. But then she placed her hand on his shoulder while he sits. Tavious stood up quickly and his system was on fire.

"Don't . . ." Tavious requested. He wanted to say more. Much louder. But he mumbled that it was enough and that he wanted to be left alone.

She moved back a few steps and was surprised that he didn't say more. She expected that he would have had said more to her. She was ready to hear it all. She was more than ready to tell her side. She couldn't wait to inform him that when he was eighteen she finally opened her eyes from the distance they shared and noticed that he was always with money. Had a car without a job. She was scared for him. She wanted to remind him that she promised God that if he was caught selling drugs she would have killed herself first before she would see him locked up like an animal in a cage. She wanted to remind him that she told him that. She wanted to enlighten him and thought he should know that Amara kept her informed of his well-being more than he would ever know during those twenty years behind bars.

Another minute had passed by now. All silence. She was in tears thinking about the things she did wrong up to this point regarding her son. All the years she spent chasing men.

Just every freakin' thing she did wrong.

"Are you just going to stand there?" she asked.

Tavious felt a spike. The uncontrollable spike that was spoken about in his counseling sessions in prison. He smiles and suppresses it for a few more minutes but just has to let it go.

"You think it's that easy? I'm standing here pushing forty years old and haven't laid eyes on you in twenty— and what? You want a kiss and a hug?"

Tavious turned around slowly and for the first time he looked at his mom only because she didn't respond. It was his first good look at her. No darkness. After all this time. He noticed the tears rolling down her face. She is twenty years older but her eyes hadn't changed a bit. Tavious focused on the tear tumbling down her cheek. Her eyes looked exactly the same as the day she dropped him off at his grandmother's to live a better life when he was seven.

Mrs. Bullock had been just outside the kitchen in the dining room, listening to every word. The room still had the oak wood cabinet record player with the vintage Stevie Wonder albums and Jackson 5 forty-five discs on the bottom shelf that they would listen to back in the day.

Tavious was exhausted by now. He didn't want to say the wrong thing. He could see her pain but still he wanted to say everything. He couldn't dismiss the words from his mouth of everything that was on his mind. It wouldn't be productive. It was against the rules of staying cool, calm, and focused. His mother doesn't move or speak. She was ready for his onslaught of words. She is tight, as though she had been sitting on death row for years. She wanted to hear it all. They stand eye to eye waiting for what was next.

Suddenly there was a never-forgettable crackle, hiss, pop, and scratching sound that could have only come from the needle on a vinyl record on the old but functional oak wood record player. It was Mrs. Bullock's favorite song, by James Cleveland, "Peace, Be Still."

Part 2

Chapter 32

I was surprised to see Tavious walk into the shop Monday morning with his mother and her husband Ely. They followed him over to his bay and from my office it looked as though he was giving them the royal tour. When they made it over to my office they were all smiles.

His mother extended her hand out to me. "West, thanks for putting Tavious in charge of your lean program," she said.

I let her know it was my pleasure right after Tavious winked his eye at me.

"You sure have a nice shop here," Ely said. "If you're ever in need of a guard dog I'm your man," he let me know.

Tavious said good-bye to them a few minutes later and when they were out the door he followed me into my office. I sat behind my desk and Tavious took the chair directly in front of my desk.

"Sometimes you have to let some things go, West," Tavious said. "All these years, man, and no matter how mad I thought I was . . . A moment can put you in a place where you can move on and live life."

I smiled at him and nodded my head in agreement. I knew exactly where Tavious's head was because Mrs. Bullock had called me bright and early just to let me know that he was in a better place.

"So, you talk to Grands?"

I nodded again.

"She thinks I need to go talk to this reporter named Saadia Eussit because she wrote an article about Amara's death."

"Couldn't hurt. But what do you think about it?"

Tavious swiped at his face and exhaled. "I don't know, man. I don't know this woman. What if she is working with the police, trying to get some kind of statement out of me."

"Well, when you talk to her it's almost going to be like a statement."

Tavious pointed toward me. "Exactly."

"What if you tell her you'll speak with her off the record?" I told him. "That way, they can't use anything you say."

Tavious kept his eyes on me and decided that he could do that, but very cautiously.

I asked him, "When does she want to meet?"

"Grands set it up for later today after work at Gladys Knight's downtown. You're going with me right?"

Chapter 33

Aa usual, the restaurant was packed. Mrs. Bullock and Saadia Eussit couldn't have picked a better place to meet because I hadn't had a bite of chicken and waffles and an ice-cold sweet tea in much too long. The restaurant was the type of establishment where you didn't make reservations, but Mrs. Bullock told us to give the head waitress our name. With the quickness they led us back to a table where a lady was sitting, wearing a blue blouse and black pants, with a notebook sitting in front of her. We presumed her to be Ms. Eussit and we were right.

After she introduced herself, Ms. Eussit let us know up front the "U" in her name was silent—"Esit"—and she was not there for any small talk by getting straight to business. We barely had a chance to sit down before she started in. By chance I noticed Tavious gawking at her iPad.

"So, I understand"—she looked at me then Tavious—"that you wanted to see me," she said. She was already in her notebook and we hadn't said a word.

Tavious answered. "I'm Tavious and this is—"

I cut him off. "My name is Pete," I informed her. There was no way she was getting any information about me. I had never read my own name in the newspaper except on a small ad in the paper about my shop, and that's the way I wanted to keep it.

The light-skinned woman peered over her reading glasses at me. "Uh . . . okay, right." She adjusted her glasses, then looked at Tavious still peering over her lenses. "You wanted to talk about the murder of Amara, I take it?"

Tavious paused, then he cleared his throat. "Yeah, yeah, that's it. I wanted to tell you . . . Wait a minute, this is off the record—right?"

She confirmed with a nod, then Tavious looked at me before he continued.

"Well, yeah, I knew her. I spoke to her while I was in prison. We were supposed to meet up when I got out but I never got a chance to talk to her."

The reporter had an oversized black leather carry bag with her and we watched as she dug into it deep. She finally brought out a folder. She looked at me for a brief second, then quickly at Tavious before reading something inside. "Do you have a phone number with the last four 6767?"

Immediately that number stood out to me as being his cell.

Tavious was close to answering. "Uhh . . ."

I cut in. "Nope." Tavious was so green to technology and knew absolutely nothing about how numbers could be traced. I just couldn't let him put himself out there like that.

Tavious looked at me and so did the reporter.

"Okay . . ." she said.

"Good," I said back.

She gave me a sharp look, then put her attention back on Tavious. "So, tell me about the relationship you had with Amara."

Tavious began to speak again. And once again I cut him off. "They were friends," I told her. "Nothing more, nothing less." I gave Tavious a nudging look to tell her more during the brief pause in the conversation, because I was sure Saadia Eussit had had enough of my interruptions even though I couldn't care less.

"Umm, yeah, he's right. We were friends. I knew her before I went to prison and we stayed in touch," Tavious explained to her.

"Only a friendship?"

"That's all it was," Tavious responded.

"So, you two didn't have any type of disagreements pertaining to anything?"

Tavious shook his head no. "Like what?"

"You tell me."

"No, we didn't." Tavious was very blunt.

"The police said her death was caused by beating and shot to the back of the head. Do you know who or why somebody would want to hurt her? Did she ever tell you someone was a threat to her?"

"Never. We talked all the time and she never said anything like that to me."

"And you talked to her how?"

"Over the phone," Tavious said.

"Over your cell phone?"

"Let me interject. You mean while you were in prison—right?"

Tavious shot me a look. "Right. That's right."

Once again the reporter tightened her eyes toward me.

Tavious turned to her. "Look, I didn't come down here to answer a bunch of questions. You're almost like the police," he tells her. "The only reason I'm here is to tell you that I didn't have anything to do with the murder of Amara. She was my friend," he said. "I wanted to let you know this firsthand because I knew it was only a matter of time before you found out that the police questioned me, and I don't want my name in one of those news articles you write."

"Well, I had that bit of information already, Tavious," she said.

"So, why didn't you print it?" I asked.

"I've been around the block a time or two, Pete. That is your name?"

"Yeah, you got it," I hit back.

"Well, Pete, I know when APD is jerking me around. They gave up his name too easy. They were trying to play me into putting his name in the paper to add pressure. I rarely do such a thing—matter of fact, I've only done it once and I was more than sure I was right," she tells us. Saadia removed her grandma, professor, really stuck-up, reading glasses from her face. It was the first time that we could see that she wasn't bad looking—beautiful even. She picked up her phone. "I just remembered, I have to make a call," she said, then got up from her seat and walked near the restroom to make her call.

Tavious followed her with his eyes. "Okay, you can go now," he told me in a low tone, almost whispering.

"What?"

He looked around the restaurant. "Yeah, you should leave now, West."

"What are you talking about?" I asked him again. I looked over at the reporter and she was deep into her call. "Are you crazy? She will eat you alive if I leave you two alone."

Tavious's tone was still lower than normal. "Don't count on it. I'm going to say very little."

"Tavious, what are you talking about?"

"She needs to know that I don't need you here to be a buffer, man. C'mon, I'll catch the train back or something," he declared.

I looked at Tavious, then back at the reporter. "Are you sure?"

"West, I got this, man."

Chapter 34

When Saddia Eussit the reporter extraordinaire returned to the table she was ready to get back to business.

She noticed within seconds. "Where's Pete?" Her tone was very sarcastic.

"Oh, he had another meeting. He's a real busy man," Tavious said. "So, I guess it's just you and me."

Saadia put her glasses back on then wrote down something in her notebook. She looked at Tavious over the rims of her glasses. "Do you think you're up to it?"

Tavious smiled for the first time and she noticed. "A man who has nothing to hide is up for anything."

Tavious left the restaurant feeling better than he did going in about his conversation with the reporter. There wasn't a question that Saadia asked that he didn't answer that could have implicated him in the murder.

Ms. Eussiet was especially interested in their relationship. Tavious didn't mind answering those questions because in his mind there was nothing to tell.

Tavious realized without delay that the reporter's angle was to show that Amara was murdered because some mad, deranged fool was madly in love with her and became upset about something and therefore killed her. But Tavious knew better and let her travel down her own road. He knew it was the two million for sure that killed his friend. When Saadia asked Tavious if he thought she was in love with him, it was really the first time he thought about it instead of dismissing it. He disclosed that it could have been a possibility even though she never directly said that she was.

When Saadia didn't let go of the love-behind-bars angle Tavious wanted to know if she was writing a romance novel instead of newspaper articles. He mentioned he was probably blind to Amara's feelings being behind prison walls. He proclaimed without glorifying any aspect of his twenty years behind bars that he was more worried about watching his back than being in love with someone on the outside he couldn't see whenever he wanted.

Soon after, Saadia began talking about her own career and some of her articles that had both helped put criminals behind bars and free some others just as well. Her degree from Penn State and the graduate work she did there was what got her thirsty for investigative reporting.

Chapter 35

Later the same night Tavious was sleeping in his new apartment above the shop and his phone rang. It sounds off a second time then a third until he was able to get his body to move. Around the eighth or ninth ring he finally picked it up and barely answered.

"Are you sleeping?"

Tavious tried to look at his alarm clock but his eyes won't focus. He stretched his arms above his head with the phone still in his hand, then moved it back down to his ear. "Of course I am; tomorrow's Monday," he struggled to say. He swiped his eyes, trying to focus on the red numbers on his clock; he faintly noticed it was eleven-something.

"So, can you meet me for coffee . . ." he heard a woman's voice sing.

"What? Who is this?"

"It's Saadia."

Even though he wasn't functioning properly, for some reason he can tell she was smiling on the other end of the phone.

"Just to let you know," she said, "this is quite frankly out the box for me, but I really would like some company."

"I've already told you all I know." Tavious looked over at the clock again and can see it a little clearer now: eleven-fifteen. He tried to count the hours he had left for rest. "Listen, I need to get some rest—"

She jumped in and stopped Tavious. "Let's be clear, Tavious. This isn't about the murder, it's about me. I will be at Café Intermezzo for an hour or so. Come see me . . . please."

Then the phone went dead. Tavious fell back down into the pillow and finally pushed the button on the phone to disconnect the call after he heard the dial tone. Tavious was no stranger to being awakened in the middle of the night, as the prison guards would get their kicks out of waking up the prisoners at all times of the night and tearing up a cell, looking for anything that wasn't supposed to be there.

Tavious was awake now. He began to debate the pros and cons of her request. A meeting with a smoking-hot news reporter who insisted the meeting was strictly about her was much too intriguing, almost unbelievable. But then again maybe she had found a discrepancy in his story and planned on setting him up when his mind was not completely clear, the same way the police interrogated him in the middle of the night over twenty years ago right before they charged him.

Whatever her reason Tavious called a cab and was downtown close to thirty minutes later. When he walked in, he was surprised to see so many people out on a Sunday night. He spotted Saadia deep in a corner alone. She had just placed her coffee cup up to her lips when she noticed him.

Tavious walked over and was taken aback when Saadia stood to give him a healthy hug. She tells him, "I was beginning to think you weren't coming."

Tavious looked around the café to see if anyone out of the ordinary may be looking at him then back at Saadia. She smiled right back at him.

"Have you been drinking anything besides that coffee?" he wanted to know.

She shook her head no. "What, would you rather I put my glasses back on and ask you some more questions or something? Sit, let's enjoy."

Tavious looked around again then pulled his chair out and sat down. The waiter came over and Tavious asked for house coffee.

"Relax, Tavious," Saadia pushed. "I figured you would be a little uptight meeting me here. Quite frankly it's kind of cute. I'm sure you're not used to a grown and sexy woman calling you in the middle of the night to talk are you?"

Tavious didn't respond. He was still trying to get over the difference in Saadia Eussit the reporter who had turned into someone different. Very different.

"To be honest with you . . ." She paused as the waiter set his drink down. "To be honest with you, your experience over the last twenty years has sparked my interest," she divulged.

Tavious smiled at her more like unbelieving of what she seemed to be selling.

"So, tell me, how does it really feel to be out of that prison with all those big, sweaty, grimy men?"

Chapter 36

The morning started off extra busy and all hands were on deck except Tavious. There was a car sitting in his bay, idle. I called upstairs to his apartment at least three times before I had to stop what I was doing to see where he was. As I was walking up the stairs a woman who looked just like Ms. Saadia Eussit was walking down the steps, smoothing out her clothes and patting down her full, fluffy but short haircut on her head. She seemed to be in even more of a rush than I was. I moved aside on the steps and gave her the right of way.

"Hey, Pete," she said without missing a beat.

I watched her sashay down the steps leading to the parking lot then get in her car and drive away. The door to the apartment was still open and I noticed Tavious standing in his underwear without a shirt.

"Good morning," he said, with the biggest smile I have ever seen on a grown-ass man.

Chapter 37

Rossi just so happened to be in my office when I went back down into the shop.

"What's wrong, bro? You look flustered."

I moved behind my desk and told him all was good. I could feel Rossi following me with wondering eyes. I begged him not to ask. I picked up the morning parts list, approved it with a quick glance, and called out to the shop to let them know it was ready.

Rossi got a bottle of water out of my refrigerator then cracked it open. "Look, man, the trail on this two million dollars is as cold as this water. No talk, no chat, nothing. I've canvassed my poker games about it so much that I'm beginning to get strange looks. Maybe that money is long gone by now."

After what I'd just witnessed upstairs in the apartment I didn't know what to think anymore. *Tavious and the reporter getting it on?* It was definitely not part of the plan to clear his name or at the least not have it placed in the paper during the police investigation. My first instinct when I saw her with her coy little smile was that she had gotten some information from Tavious that she couldn't wait to get into the next edition of the paper.

When I finally get Rossi off my back Tavious walks in my office wearing jeans. His shirt was buttoned halfway and his shoes were untied.

Rossi scanned him over once he walked in. "Problems getting dressed, T?"

Tavious blew him off and looked directly at me. "West, it just happened. She called me last night, asked me to meet her for a second time. We had coffee, chatted, and the next thing I knew we were back at my place, buck-naked nonstop, until five minutes before you came up to check on me," he said.

Rossi's eyes perked up. "Aww, shit, this is my type of conversation."

"The reporter, Tavious?" That's all I could say.

"The reporter you guys met with last night?" Rossi wanted to know.

"The one and only," I tell him.

Rossi looked at me then at Tavious.

"Man, it's been over twenty years—what do you expect me to do, turn it down?"

"You got a point there," Rossi said. "So, is it true, you never forget?" Rossi smiled.

Tavious smiled almost in remembrance. "Never, man. Believe that."

"Let's try to forget about the sex and focus. Did you tell her anything that can get you put in jail? I can't believe you just slept with the reporter investigating the case of a murder that you have been questioned about."

Tavious said, "Nothing. There was very little talking." Then he smiled.

"My man . . ." Rossi interjected. "Look, it may not be that bad," Rossi said. "At least now he can keep an eye on her just as much as she can him. You have to work this to your advantage, man. Get her on your side."

I could understand where Rossi was coming from.

"I don't know. This lady is fire," Tavious said. "Why would I waste the chance of being with her, trying to keep her close to me, when I might want to be with her?"

"Be with her?" I questioned.

Rossi pointed his bottle of water at Tavious. "Yeah, you have been locked away for twenty years," Rossi said. "Brother, trust me, a one-night stand does not mean a chick wants to be with you. It's a new day; they are as bad as us," Rossi said.

"Sometimes worse," I let him know.

Chapter 38

Tavious was wide open now. He was so excited about spending time with Saadia the reporter that he invited her to dinner with his mother and Ely the very same night.

"And you two met when?" Joyce asked the lustful couple sitting across from her after witnessing the fourth or fifth thirty-second tonsil-checking, tongue-twisting kiss shared between Saadia and Tavious.

"Last night," Tavious said; then he kisses the reporter on her lips again without hesitation.

She smiled and grabbed his ear. "Umm, actually it was yesterday, but we met again last night." She moved her hand down his neck then says, "Over and over again."

Ely hadn't said much the entire night but watching these two was priceless. The smile on his face as he watched Tavious fill up Saadia at every moment was rewarding in more ways than one. There was no doubt that she was a looker. Probably could have been a model if she wanted to with her beautiful olive skin tone. There actually hadn't been a man who walked past them who didn't notice how lovely she was.

Saadia definitely didn't disappoint socially. Sharing so much about her family background of being raised in Newark, New Jersey by a single mom and applying to Penn State on a dare was interesting stuff. Her decision to never have children and instead live life to the fullest extent with no regrets was refreshing and understandable. She told everyone when she died she wanted to say to herself *what a ride.* She had a moment though as the wine and conversation got to her. She told everyone her mother never finished high school and the struggle of keeping clothes on their backs admittedly traumatized her so much that she never wanted to have to endure that type of struggle again with a child of her own.

"So, Joyce, you get two thumbs up for putting this dinner together," she lets her know.

Joyce and Ely smile. Proud. Carrabba's Italian Grill was one of their favorite places to eat. They were happy that everyone was enjoying themselves.

"This just shows how deep love is. Nothing, not even twenty years can keep loved ones apart. Simply amazing," Saadia believed.

Joyce smiled. She almost let her guard down to talk about Amara but quickly decided against it. She was not as willing to let Saadia in as quickly as Tavious and overly admiring Ely. She wasn't clear of her intentions. For all she knows she was willing to give up anything to pin the murder of Amara on her son.

When the reporter excused herself to the ladies' room Joyce made her thoughts known without any hesitation. She double-checked to make sure the reporter was nowhere around before she spoke on it. "Tavious?"

Tavious looked up from his drink with a smile on his face.

"What is going on with this woman? You mean to tell me you have hooked up with the reporter investigating the murder?"

Tavious smiled again. "Well, by the way it's going it sure is a possibility," he mentioned.

Ely clinched his fist and gave Tavious a pound.

"No, no, you fools. You don't know her from Adam. She might be setting you up."

"Setting me up?"

"That's right."

"How can she set me up when I didn't do anything?" Ely interrupted. "He has a point there. If you are innocent, walking around like it and having her on your arm is at least telling anyone who thinks otherwise that you're not hiding a damn thing," he said.

This time Tavious initiated the pound.

"I'm just saying it's different out here now; plus, you've never ever been in a relationship," Joyce schooled.

"At least not with a woman," Ely joked.

Tavious is feeling too good at this point to get upset and waves Ely off. "I know the guys at the shop already told me, but I trust her; she's cool."

"Well, at least try to keep what you tell her to a minimum. Especially anything about me."

"You?"

"Yes, me—have you forgotten that I went over to see Amara right before you found out that she was dead? I don't want her asking me questions about anything because if she wrote that in the paper the police would think I had something to do with it."

"Look, I promise you, she's not like that. She doesn't even know you knew Amara and that's the way I plan on keeping it. Besides, we haven't talked about that since we first met. We are on a whole different level. This has much more to do with than an investigation."

Tavious tried to assure his mother with his eyes. When she turned away he smiled at Ely.

Ely motioned with a nudge that Saadia was on her way back to the table.

Joyce was not buying it, not just yet, and she looked around at Tavious and Ely with disapproval of the way they were gawking over Saadia. In her mind Saadia had them both wrapped around her pinky finger.

Chapter 39

Eeven though Tavious wanted to get back to Saadia and enjoy some intense time alone, he halfheartedly agreed to have a nightcap over at Ely and his mother's place. Ely and Joyce were good together. There was no denying the honeymoon phase for beginning couples was over but they were truly into each other. Even Saadia mentioned how respectfully they spoke to one another, always sure to say please and thank you.

Their home was north up in Henry County down on a country road, but still close enough to the city of Atlanta where they could reach the city in twenty-five minutes if needed. Tavious was impressed at first glance but didn't see ever coming out this way in the middle of the night. The roads were dark, houses spaced much too far apart for his taste; the driveway leading up to the house almost half a mile long, surrounded by nothing but trees and brush. Once they reached a certain point motion detectors picked up movement and lights were turned on all around and inside the house. Ely stopped his truck and when they got out they could hear dogs barking in the rear of the house.

They all looked at the house illuminating. It was a three-story all-brick structure that looked to have at least four bedrooms inside. It seemed as though every light in the house was turned on by the monitors.

"If I lived out here, I would have my house light up just like this when I come home," Saadia mentions. "Living way out here in these woods you have to be extra careful."

"Joyce made me do it," Ely said, as he pulled his visor down from the outside of the truck and mashes on another button that opened up the garage. "It took her at least two months before she became comfortable living out here."

"That's right. Even with all those dogs back there you hear hollering like they don't have any sense, I'm still scared sometimes," she teases.

"Wow, how many dogs back there?" Tavious wanted to know.

"Oh . . . I don't know. Depends on if the litter I've been waiting on is ready," Ely said.

"Puppies?" Saadia wants to know.

"Hopefully so," Ely wanted. "Let's go back and check."

Joyce started walking into the garage. "Uh-uh, not me. I will have to wait until the morning."

Saadia is right behind her. "I think I'll pass too." She chuckled.

Ely looked at Tavious. "Well, I guess that leaves just you and me."

Chapter 40

"All I know is good loving makes you do some strange things."

"You should know," Rita said to Rossi without even looking up from her hand of cards while we played a game of spades.

"I just hope he knows what he's doin'," Lauren added.

"Seems to be pretty sure of himself," I let them know right before I threw down an ace of diamonds under gasps of disappointment to earn my team another book.

It was almost unbelievable that Saadia, the hall of fame reporter, had it bad for Tavious and he'd actually taken her out with his mother and her husband Ely for a meet and greet. Rita and Lauren used their women's perspective on the situation and were adamant that a woman could not actually fall for a man so quickly, especially if they found him intriguing.

Rossi agreed with me that there was no way a woman would take up so much interest in a man if she wasn't trying to get something from him. Rita thought that the reporter probably had some kind of fetish for being with a man who'd been locked up.

No matter what our opinions on the matter were, Tavious was treading lightly in a world he didn't know anything about with Saadia, in my opinion. Going from getting interviewed to getting laid was too much of a stretch for me. I didn't want to see him get into a situation he couldn't get out of by saying the wrong things to her. But he was a grown man able to do as he pleased, even though I promised Mrs. Bullock that I would keep the situation under control. This wasn't under control.

For the next several hours while Rita and Rossi were enjoying the thorough whipping they were placing on us in spades, our conversation remained on Tavious and what his mindset could have been trying to deal with the reporter. I would have imagined him having major trust issues because of being just released from prison. But everyone else was in agreement that feelings, emotion, and sex trumped anything else that may have been going on in his mind, and that's why at the moment he was someplace with Saadia getting all those needs met that had been abandoned the last twenty years.

We were basically going through the motions of the last hand because the game was pretty much over, and just when I nonchalantly threw the queen of spades out to overtake the ten of spades, even though I had a jack, there was a loud knock at the door which basically froze us all.

"Police! Open this got-damn door," is what came after the pounding on my not-yet-one-month-old solid mahogany wood door.

"What the hell is going on?" Rossi stood up from the card table not knowing what to expect next.

I went over to my window that gave a direct line of sight to the front of the house, then looked out and saw what looked like no fewer than six police cars and one dog. I let everyone inside know that it was in fact the police and to be cool.

I looked over at Rita and Lauren and they were already visibly shaken by the intrusion. Rossi stood with his hands in his pockets and motioned for me to answer the door. As I walked over to the door there was another loud pound, then instructions to open the door again. I looked back at everyone, and as soon as I unlocked the door it was pushed open, and a white piece of paper was shoved in my face and fell to the ground before I could read it.

"Warrant, motherfucka." It was Officer Williams, his partner Gus, and at least four other grimy cops who had made their way inside.

"What's this about?" I asked.

"Raid," Williams said.

"For what?" Rossi wanted to know.

"Read the warrant, got-damn it," Gus said to Rossi.

When Rossi reached down to pick it off the floor he was told by another officer not to fuckin' move.

"You just can't come up in here like this," Lauren said.

"We did. And we are," Williams said to her in a smart tone; then I saw his eyes travel over her body. Lauren moved back a bit, feeling uncomfortable.

I was getting upset with the entire situation. "Okay, so you are. What are you looking for?"

"Money," Williams said. "two million dollars cash, so if you have anything like that up in here it would behoove your meddling-in-police-business ass to tell us now. If not, according to that warrant signed by the judge, in exactly twenty seconds we have the right to tear this place up, and believe me when I tell you, you will not recognize this place when we're done."

When Williams mentioned the two million we all knew what he was talking about but we didn't know where it was either. There was no reason to even acknowledge that we even knew about the money because if we had, he would have taken us all downtown and had us in questioning the entire night.

So we kept our mouths shut, and just like the scumbag officer promised they commenced tearing my house apart, looking for the two million. When I asked the reason why they would think we had two million stashed in our home, I was told that I have been consorting with an ex-felon and they have reason to believe the friendship and employment have turned into criminal actions and activity.

I knew it was bullshit, and Lauren was devastated watching them tear up our new home, which she decorated top to bottom. The officers pulled up our rugs in several rooms, tore through drywall, broke several tables, punched holes in our ceilings and cut through every mattress in the house.

Rossi had seen enough and began to get upset with the officers, and Williams told him not to worry; his place more than likely would be next if he didn't shut the hell up. Three hours later they finally left, promising to come back as many times as needed to retrieve the millions of dollars they claim should have been turned in when Tavious was arrested twenty years ago.

Chapter 41

Still out in the country suburb, Tavious and Ely stepped out of Ely's truck and approached what looked to be at least fifteen dog runs sitting behind the house less than seventy-five meters away. The dog runs were well lit just like the house. There was not a problem seeing the setup at all. At first glance each metal fence run looked to have at least three to four dogs inside with the same amount of housing.

"Geez, man, how many you got back here?" Tavious was amazed.

"The last count I had twenty-six, but who knows now because I've been waiting on my prime bitch to do what she does best." Ely nudged Tavious on the shoulder and led him past the barking dogs in the runs and into a concrete structure that looked as though he had built it himself. It was completely concrete cylinder blocked on the outside and had concrete flooring on the inside. He had four different doors inside and they were all closed, except the one leading to a room where there was a desk, television, and a few chairs. He clicked on the lights to the office. "Welcome to E Kennels," he said with extended arms.

After the long fluorescent lights on the ceiling fought through the flickering process of turning completely on and lighting the room, Tavious was able to focus his eyes on posters of dogs with the name E KENNELS placed on the top of each one. Tavious took his time looking at the posters on the wall under the watchful eye of Ely, who was standing proud as though he would never get tired of seeing them. The dogs in the photos didn't look like some high-profile massive killers that could tear you a new one. The pictures of the dogs were simply showing their beauty.

Tavious pointed at one poster. "Rottweiler, right?"

"That's right, one of my best ever," Ely mentioned.

Tavious walked closer to the poster right next to the Rott. "But this one here? What kind of dog is this? He's fuckin' beautiful."

"That's Randolph, a champion Cane Corso."

"Cane Corso?" Tavious repeated.

"Yeah, an Italian Mastiff."

"He's huge . . ."

"A hell of a dog—there was a point in time when the only type of dog I would breed was the Rottweiler . . ."

"Why's that?"

"I love 'em, man, and they do have a way of making money. They are excellent guard dogs, family dogs, and companions. But check this here—one day a guy from Italy came by to check out my champion stud Rott that he wanted to take back to his home country and breed. He told me about the Cane Corso. I fell in love on sight. I couldn't believe a dog could be so beautiful. I mean, I had heard of the breed before, but you know how we are when we think what we are already doing is the best way. But after watching a tape of his dogs, I hopped my own flight to Italy, saw his dogs, and ended up doing a sign and trade for one of his champions and two sexy bitches. I have been breeding them since."

After a few more moments of looking at the rest of the posters on the wall and Ely telling him the history of each dog displayed, Ely asked Tavious to follow him. They walked through the hallway in the direction of

one of the closed doors in the concrete slab. Ely unlocked the door and they went inside.

Inside the five-by-five room was a dog that looked
very familiar to the Cane Corso breed on the poster. It
was down on the floor on a bundle of blankets. It didn't
even think about standing up on its feet when they
entered. The dog looked weak and Ely went over and
stroked its head.

"It's okay, Patty Cake," he told the dog. "You're doing
fine girl," he soothed her. "You have anything for me?"

Tavious watched closely as Ely looked down at the
end of the dog and removed a blanket and picked up
two little newborn pups that were cuddled up together.

"Oh yeah," he said. Then he looked at Patty Cake
again, who seemed like she had been through the drill a
time or two before. "That's a good girl," he calmed her.
"Only nine more, okay? The doc said you could have at
least eleven, so take your time, baby; it will be okay."

Tavious moved forward to get a better look.

Ely continued to hold the pup in his hands. "Cane
Corso pups, man. Champion bloodlines. I'm holding
over four grand in my hand."

Tavious declared, "I've never seen pups that color in
my life."

Ely looked up at Tavious from his kneeling position.
"This is what we call rare blue. These pups' pigmenta-
tion didn't come all the way through. I have two rare
blue studs out in the yard."

Tavious moved a bit closer and bent down with his
hands on his knees. Ely handed him the pup; it was a
male.

"He's yours," Ely said.

"What? Mine . . ."

"That's right, welcome home."

Chapter 42

A couple of hours had passed and the police had been long gone when I found out through Mrs. Bullock that the warrant served to search my home was a fake. Rossi was triple teed off to the umpteenth power. He wanted some get back. Rossi was ranting over and over why he didn't trust the police from the first knock on the door.

Mrs. Bullock verified to us through one of her many contacts downtown that there had been no judge whatsoever who granted a warrant to search my house. The officers were running buck wild making their own rules.

"Those motherfuckers are looking for the money just like we are, West," Rossi proclaimed. He went over to my liquor cabinet, or what was left of it.

I walked over to him, sidestepping broken glass, and poured myself a drink right along with him. "This is some bullshit, man." I took my whiskey straight down while looking at my ransacked home. "I was beginning not to care one way or another about this money since Tavious went off on his Love Boat trip. But the police are in it. There is no way I am letting those crooked bastards strong-arm their way into some dough just because they think they're entitled because of their badges."

"No doubt they are hunting for it," Rossi said. "They are descendants of Stallings and that means they are some dirty sons of bitches."

Lauren walked in the room with Rita and they both had trash bags and threw a few our way. I poured another drink and took it down much quicker than the first one. "This is about to come to a head. The police know about the money, we know about the money, and there is someone out there who has the money."

"But it seems like nobody knows who that is," Lauren said.

"And that's the way they plan on keeping it," Rossi decided.

"Well the police got their information from someplace," I remind them.

"But where?" Rita asked.

"That's the two-million-dollar question," I said.

Chapter 43

By this time Tavious and Ely had made it back into his office. Tavious thanked Ely for the pup but told him it would be difficult to travel out to where they lived to take care of him every day.

"Don't worry. I'll take care of him for you. We'll just keep him here. You come by and get acquainted from time to time. Soon enough you will fall for this dog so hard that I bet you money you'll take him home one day," Ely assured him.

Ely's words didn't seem to register. Tavious hadn't kissed his hot scribe in over twenty minutes. He was looking out the one and only window in the room that pointed toward the house, probably wondering what his mom and newfound friend in lust were talking about.

Ely picked up on his dreamlike state then collapsed down in his chair and exhaled. He seemed to be struggling with something on his mind as well. Ely stared at Tavious as his back was toward him.

Tavious started looking at the posters on the wall again.

Ely picked up a pen from his desk, tapped it on the desk a few times, then said, "Dolla Bill . . . Mad Man Jones . . . Chewy Maddaux."

Tavious turned around slowly, now engaged with Ely face to face.

Ely displayed a crooked smile then paused. "Old friends of mine," he pronounced.

"Old friends?" Tavious inquired, knowing they were high-rolling drug dealers on the streets over twenty years ago who he knew all too well. Tavious's whole demeanor changed, almost as though he realized his celly stole something from him. "What do you mean old friends?"

Ely just wouldn't stop with the pen. Tap, tap, tap . . . His expression was not quite a smile. It was more like a devious bitch-ass look. Like he for whatever reason wanted to get under Tavious's skin.

"I have another name for you before I explain myself." Ely had Tavious's full attention now.

Tavious moved closer to the desk to hear what he had to say.

Without delay, "Gully Brown," he pushed.

Tavious and Ely lock eyes like two prized fighters. Ely seemed relieved that he spilled it.

"What the fuck you talking Gully Brown—Ely? Why are you slinging his name around me?"

Ely smiled. "He's a friend of mine too." Ely sensed Tavious's inner confusion. Ely exhaled and began to clarify himself. "I grew up with him. Gully and me were good friends. Lived in the same hood, same school, everything. He just decided to go one way with his life and I went the other." Ely paused, really enjoying the moment. "Ol' Gully and me go way back. Shit, we were so close that we told a few kids back in the day we were cousins."

"Don't know what it has to do with me though," Tavious lets him know.

Ely is a bit harder now. "Well, it has a lot to do with you, you see. When you were inside, I talked to Gully the night before he called it quits and moved to Mexico.

I bet your ass he is curled up with a couple of Honey Dips, drinking that shit and living life nice and easy," he said. Ely looked like he was getting tired of his own game. He stopped tapping his pen on the desk and finally got down to business. "Look, I bought the paper you owed Gully. Now you owe me."

"Man, what the hell are you talking about?"

"The money you owed Gully, and stashed away right before you went to prison."

"Wherever you got your information done told you wrong."

"I don't think so. I got my info from Gully. Said you had the money after the pickup in Miami. It was a refund from another deal that you two did with his Cuban connect named Arturo. You used your half on more weed. But you were going to get thirty percent cash for the delivery of the money to Gully's front door. Gully figured you switched bags with someone on that bus before you were busted. But he never realized why you didn't switch the drugs, too."

Ely noticed Tavious go back in time as he wondered the same thing.

"Oh, well, doesn't matter now. It took Gully some time to figure out the police didn't seize your shit. He wasn't going to wait around twenty years for your ass to finish your bid when he already had more than enough money in the bank."

Tavious didn't say anything. Ely knew way too much info on Gully and the Cuban connect for his words to be lies but he still wasn't going to admit anything.

"Look, here's the bottom line. I purchased your debt from Gully for a fair price. You haven't been out long enough to spend the two million, so this is what I'm goin' to do."

"Yeah, what's that?"

"I'm going to let you have two hundred thousand, because that's the type of man I am. Plus, we're family, right."

"Fuck outta here," Tavious said.

Ely laughed him off. "But you only get it if you take me this very moment to pick it up."

"You must be out of your fuckin' mind," Tavious told him. "You bought a bad note—that's if you stepped to it or not. No way I'm going to let you bully me on some bullshit."

"So you're saying I'm perpetrating a fraud to get your paper?" Ely opened his desk drawer as he waited for Tavious's answer.

"That's exactly what I'm saying," Tavious shot back.

"I thought you might say that." Ely finds what he is looking for inside the desk and pulled out a piece of paper. He picked up the phone on his desk and began to dial. Tavious watched his every move. Ely pressed the phone on the side of his face and waited for his call to be answered. Then Ely smiled and pointed toward the receiver of the phone.

"Hey, I was expecting a spicy-hot mama named Maria to answer the phone." Ely kept an eye on Tavious as he listened to the response. "Guess who I have standing in front of me? Your man, Tavious Bell. That's right—he did the twenty. I caught up with him and for some reason he doesn't believe that I own his ass until he gives me the two mil I purchased from you." Ely chuckled. "Yeah, he's right here." Ely took the phone off his ear and gave it to Tavious.

Tavious snatched the phone from Ely's hand. "Tavious."

When Tavious heard the voice on the other end, there was no doubt it was Gully Brown, the man who he had done many drug deals with before. His voice was still raspy and low. Tavious listened to him explain what was going on and at the end of the conversation, Gully told him that he sold the note to Ely because he was sure that Tavious would never do the entire twenty without being killed inside.

"Well, you bet wrong," Tavious told him right before slamming the phone back on Ely's desk. Tavious gave Ely a stern look then walked out of his office and back to the house to retrieve Saadia.

Chapter 44

We heard knocking on the door again. Not as loud or intense as a few hours earlier but it was more constant. I still sent the girls upstairs and took out my heat and gave Rossi one as well. It was a Beretta Nano 9 mm.

I stood directly in front of the door and Rossi toward the side in a hallway, fully locked and loaded. I wasn't totally ready for a shoot-out. *Shit.* Mentally maybe but physically nowhere close for a battle with crooked police. I balanced my weight as best as I could and tried to focus on defending my property. I was not going to let another police officer in my home to walk around like they owned the place. I was planning for what was about to happen next to be on Fox 5 news for sure.

I checked on Rossi's position. He gave me thumbs-up. I walked up to the door and looked out the peephole. Fuck me. It was Tavious and his all-star reporter. I opened the door. They took one step into my place and looked around.

"What the fuck happened in here?" Tavious was curious to know.

Saadia grabbed on to his arm extra tight, then stepped over my oak cabinet along with broken glass that now made its home on the floor instead of against my wall. "Funny, when I met you, Pete, I didn't think you liked it rough," Saadia said.

Lauren and Rita peeked down from upstairs. I introduced Saadia to the ladies and Rossi. After we filled them in on what happened she rolled up her sleeves and began to pitch in and help out with the mess. Tavious wanted to speak with me and Rossi alone. We went outside to chat.

Tavious lit up a smoke first. "Damn night has been full of surprises hasn't it?" Tavious took a drag on his smoke. "Muthafuckas always working an angle. Being out here is no more different than being in the joint."

We didn't quite understand where he was going with what he was saying. He was actually more like mumbling, so Rossi asked him what he was talking about after he bummed a smoke.

"Got-damn Ely," he said.

"That's your mother's better half?" I asked.

"Check." Tavious took another drag on his smoke. "He purchased a note I owed back in the day on a purchase of Kush. Something I was going to pay before I was busted but it never happened."

"How much does he want?

"He wants it all. He wants it all, West."

Tavious's news was a major blow. We sat and talked about it without delay. Rossi was in agreement. There was no way we could stand in the way of a man with a verified promissory note that had been stamped in the streets in his hand. I had only laid eyes on Ely one time in the parking lot of the police station. If he showed proof that he had an agreement with this Gully Brown and the two million was his then that alone put us all out of the equation for sure because I wasn't going there.

More than anything I was pissed that I had to get back to work extra hard and get my house back in order after the police wrecked it. Rossi didn't have too much time invested but he was willing to chalk the whole experience up as a possible deal that didn't materialize. At least we were all safe and no one was injured trying to get what we all thought there was a chance of obtaining.

I was still worried about Tavious though; we all were. I didn't know what Ely had up his sleeve particularly because Tavious didn't know where the money was. Tavious was going to have to be extra careful around him because Ely had total access to his life since he was married to his mother.

Chapter 45

A few days later, Tavious was in his apartment with his mind churning on fire, realizing what he anticipated having in his hands for twenty long years had dissipated to the small sum of $200,000, and that was *only* if he was lucky enough to find out who was in possession of it.

Tavious had planned to spend the evening with Saadia but it was already seven o'clock and she hadn't called. The last time he spoke with her she was doing a half day of work then meeting with his mother for an afternoon lunch. It soothed his heart to know at least something was working out. At this time in his life a relationship would more than likely be the best thing for him.

Tavious decided it was time to give Saadia a call. As soon as he picked up his phone to dial her number his phone rang.

It was Ely. Tavious was not too happy to hear from him. "So what do you want?"

"My man. Why are you so hostile? We are not even close to being hostile. I mean we are practically family."

Tavious could hear his chuckle, which sounded as though he thought he had Tavious by the balls. "Like I said, what do you want?"

"Well . . . I thought that you might want to know that your girl is over here with your mother."

"I know that," Tavious said.

"But I don't think you know they have been going at it for the last twenty or so minutes and I am not the one to break up two women arguing."

"Arguing? About what?"

"Come find out for yourself," Ely told him; then the phone went dead.

Chapter 46

"West, I need you, man."

That's exactly what Tavious relayed to me over the phone. I could feel by his tone he was rushing. My first thought was the police were on top of his ass again.

"I need a ride out to Henry County," he pushed.

"Henry County?"

"Ely called. Said my mother and Saadia are out there in some type of tiff."

I didn't respond.

" Can you come get me and take me out there so I can see what's going on?"

I wasn't in the mood. I had just about gotten over all the time I had spent on the hunt for the two million with the help of the cognac that was staring back at me. Plus, I was still finding little pieces of broken glass on my floor.

"C'mon, now, West. I really appreciate all that you have done for me since I've been released and I know your house is busted up but . . ." There was a pause. "I just need to get out there and see what this is all about."

It was against my better judgment but I had a corner more of cognac in my glass and took it straight down. "I'm on my way."

As we ventured out to Henry County, Tavious promised to wash and wax my ride on the next picture-perfect day. He still couldn't get over the fact that Mrs.

Bullock gave me his grandfather's prized car. I think Tavious asking to wash it was his chance to go back down memory lane a bit and think about old times, the days before he was locked up.

Except for a little bit of traffic on Interstate 285 we were able to make good time. Tavious estimated it was about thirty minutes or so since he last chatted with Ely and he was a bit worried because each time he called Saadia's or his mother's number the phones were not being answered.

When we arrived Tavious went ahead of me. I was lagging behind, taking cautious steps, checking out the spread and wondering why I was hearing so many dogs. Their barking was so loud I wondered if any were wandering loose. I damn sure heard what seemed to be thousands on the grounds.

Tavious glanced back at me. He was already standing at the front door.

"C'mon, man, it's cool. Those dogs are locked up," he said.

"You sure?"

"Nah, but you better not be on the outside of this door if they're not. Just saying, 'cause I saw a few nasty sons of bitches the last time I was out here and they don't play."

I didn't know if Tavious was serious but I was not taking any chances. For the first time in years I moved my legs with the quickness with a quick step up to the front door. I stood right beside Tavious, keeping my eye out for anything that approached me with four legs attached to its body.

Tavious knocked twice. We could faintly hear shouting, maybe an argument, but because of the dogs barking we weren't sure.

Tavious looked at me. "What you wanna do, West?"

"Hey, I'm here for you," I let him know.

We were standing, looking at one another. It was his family, his girl, his decision.

Tavious said, "Fuck it." Then he opened the door and we walked in.

We were just inside the door of the house with the open floor plan. It seemed to be an oversized ranch, perfect for living out in the country in all the sticks and trees. The house was cleaned to perfection, quite a contrast to mine since the police visit. It took only a few seconds to realize that the shouting voices we thought we had heard outside the door were a matter of fact. We didn't rush to the location of the shouting as we didn't know what to expect. But as we got closer we could almost figure it out through all the screaming and yelling.

"Let's just get one thing clear, you tell-it-all scribe! My son is not ready for a relationship with you—bitch! He's been locked up for twenty years so of course he thinks he likes you. Yes . . . everyone knows why he's so taken by you—you're a freakin' slut!"

"You can't tell me who I can or cannot see! I don't care if Tavious is your son, I'm going to be with him as long as he wants to be with me—so open this fuckin' door, bitch. I'm not telling you again!"

When we located the spot where the screaming was coming from Joyce was standing with her back on a wall, looking up at the ceiling of the house. It was obvious what was going on. When Joyce turned her head and saw us standing there she took a deep breath and nothing more.

"Ma?" Tavious was perplexed. She didn't answer. "Ma?"

She took another deep sigh.

"What's going on? Where is Saadia?"

"Tavious? Tavious, is that you?" Saadia said from behind a door. "Tavious, your crazy-ass mother has locked me up in this bathroom and won't let me out. I wanted to call you, but she has my phone and keys."

"That's right— sure do and I'm going to keep them until you understand that I am not going to let you set my son up and take the fall for Amara's death. I know that's what this is all about anyway. Put two and two together. You do a story on her death and all of sudden you're sleeping with the unnamed police suspect."

"Ma, what's wrong with you? You can't keep her in there," Tavious testified.

"That's right, let me outta here," we hear Saadia shout.

Tavious walked a few steps to the door. "C'mon, that's enough let her out. You two were supposed to have lunch, not get into it," Tavious rationalized.

"I did try to hang out with her, but when I came in to use the bathroom before I left I heard the door lock behind me," Saadia lets him know.

Joyce didn't say anything; she just looked back toward the sound of Saadia's voice.

I didn't know what to think of the situation. I was surprised, though, that a grown-ass woman locked another in a bathroom because she was sleeping with her son.

Tavious walked over to the door and grabbed the doorknob and pushed the door. It didn't open. He looked over at his mother. "You have a deadbolt on a bathroom door?"

"Crazy-ass bitch!" Saadia screamed out.

"Yes, Ely put the deadbolt on it. He uses it sometimes when his prime bitches are in heat and he gets concerned sometimes that someone will try to steal them and he keeps them in there. So I decided to use it for this bitch."

Tavious took a deep breath after looking at me, shaking his head. He held out his hand in his mother's direction. "Keys please?"

"Don't have them," she said.

"What do you mean you don't have them!" Saadia screamed.

Tavious pushed out his hand again, waiting for keys.

"Ely has them. He's out back," she said.

"How are you going to lock me in the bathroom without the keys?" Saadia said through the door.

Tavious looked at me as the ladies continued their back and forth.

"C'mon, West, let's go get these keys."

"Those dogs back there?" I wanted to know.

Tavious had already started to walk down the hallway. "Yeah."

"That's okay—I'm good," I told him then I threw him my keys because he said he didn't want to walk back to the kennels in the dark.

Chapter 47

Tavious was overly hesitant opening the door and walking into the kennel. He took about two steps inside before he called out Ely's name. No answer. He called again. No answer. Then he called out to him a third time. There was still no answer. Ely probably couldn't hear him because the dogs' volume inside was almost deafening with the cinderblock acoustics bouncing off the walls.

Tavious could see the office with the posters from where he stood and decided to walk back. As soon as he placed one foot inside the room he was greeted by a ferocious dog that stood at the ready in attacking position. Tavious was stunned. He couldn't take his eyes off the dog's gigantic head and reaching teeth as it barked nonstop. Its slobber foam around its mouth and growling were enough to make anyone concede. Ely was sitting behind his desk, tapping that damn pen on it, with a huge smile on his face.

"Don't look him in the eye," Ely instructed over the commotion. "If you do, I don't know if I will be able to get him off you."

The dog continued his discomfort with Tavious. Its stand was forceful and strong begging Tavious to make a move.

"Get the dog, man," Tavious ordered. Tavious was looking across at the posters on the wall again.

"You got my money?" Ely inquired.

"I already told you, I don't have it and I don't know who does."

Tavious could feel the dog inching closer to him in the small office just because he could and Ely was not giving it instructions not to.

"I'm telling you, man, get the dog," Tavious said again with a nervous laugh.

Ely stands up and shouts, "Or what! What are you going to do?"

By now Tavious was furious and didn't say another word until Ely finished with his laughter of Tavious standing there defenseless with his dog letting out his aggression. Finally, after what seems like hours, Ely placed his fingers in his mouth and whistled. The dog stopped barking immediately and ran to his side. With a coy smile on his face Ely placed the leash on its choker chain around the dog's neck, then walked past Tavious out the door.

Tavious heard him place the dog behind a nearby gate while all along praising the dog for acting like the devil.

Ely returned like nothing happened but surely he could see the sweat on the crest of Tavious's brow.

"So, I guess you're here to get the key—right?"

"Right," Tavious answered.

Chapter 48

When Tavious came back with the key I was pretty much going back and forth from watching a show about housewives who live in Atlanta and listening to the ladies screaming at one another through the bathroom door. There was not that much difference in the two and both were getting on my damn nerves.

Tavious didn't say a word when he walked past me and toward the locked door but I did hear him huff a few times like he was agitated. Saadia called out to him as she heard the key begin to negotiate the lock. When it was open she came out. She looked around while running her hand through her hair and took a deep breath.

Joyce was standing close with piercing eyes but not close enough where she could get punched.

"You are lucky I don't press charges against your stupid ass," Saadia told her.

"Okay, let's go," Tavious told Saadia.

"No, we need to address this," Saadia said.

Tavious began to push her by her waist. "No, we don't—let's go. You ready, West?"

Joyce wouldn't stop. "Yeah, get her outta here, so I can take me a bath," Joyce said. "Get all this filth off me from standing too close to her."

Tavious was literally pushing Saadia by the waist out the door. He couldn't get out of the house quick enough.

"Yeah, right, bitch, you're the only one dirty up in here," Saadia said back. "I'm a grown-ass woman; you don't lock me up in your house!" Saadia didn't waste any time leaving the house. She jumped in her car without another word.

Tavious thought about calling her on the ride back home but decided he was going to give her some time. On the drive back Tavious didn't have much to say.

"Man, don't sweat it," I told him. "You've missed the entire revolution of women while you were locked up. Women today say what's on their mind and they make sure it's heard. There's no way you could have seen that coming. Your mother is just watching your back because, after all, Saadia is a reporter and they haven't put that case to bed yet," I let him know.

"I get all that, man—but Ely is going to have to be dealt with."

I looked over at Tavious as I made a left-hand turn.

"West, that fool tried to play me tonight," he said.

"How's that?"

"When I went back to the kennels to get the key, he put one of his dogs on me."

I quickly looked Tavious over because I hadn't noticed him acting as though he had been hurt in any way.

"No, no, I'm good. But when I walked in the office he put the dog in a ready position, to attack me."

"So, what happened?"

"He called the dog off but not before he asked about the money again. The money that I don't have."

"So, what'd you tell him?"

"Not much, West. I just made sure he locked that dog gate back up and got the key from him to unlock the door. After that I let him know that he should have never, ever done that to me."

Chapter 49

Rossi had already let it be known that he was going to continue with his incessant hustle of playing poker and taking his winnings and losings with a grain of salt. But this night his card game losses were bigger than usual. All he wanted to do was get home. His close-to-drunken stroll through the parking lot back to his BMW was met with surprise. He faintly hears hollow-sounding words in the garage of a controlled ruckus nearby.

"You're going to keep your mouth shut, motherfuc-ka—do you understand?" Rossi overheard followed by two hard, echoing slaps and reacted grunts.

It wasn't long before Rossi could focus on the commotion. Two men were standing over a man. He was doubled over, holding his stomach, trying to find the air to answer his assailants. They were about fifteen steps away from Rossi's car.

"Seems like he don't wanna answer, Mac," one of the men said.

Rossi could only see the back of their bodies. The men giving out the beating were standing, looking down at their victim. Without provocation they started whaling on the defenseless man again. This time Rossi could see the punches being delivered. Some of the punches were to his head. The others were flush against his body, making a thumping sound when they landed. When the men stopped to admire their body of work they chatted between themselves while the beaten man on the ground hacked and coughed. He spit out blood, too.

Rossi unlocked his car doors, which made his alarm device do a double screeching sound that echoed through the parking garage. The two men turned around and noticed Rossi, who still hadn't taken his eyes off the action.

"Hey, man, what're you lookin' at?" one of the men asked.

This time Rossi could see a bit of his face through the somewhat dark light. He was white with a full head of hair. He was wearing a suit. He had bulging eyes. Rossi only noticed because he was trying to stare Rossi down.

The other man turned away from looking at Rossi. He was black and had on a suit too. He didn't care and went back to work and punched the already-beaten man again. Then he looked back at Rossi. "Oh—you lookin' at that?" He punched him again and again while the man lay coughing. He stopped, asked for a light for his smoke dangling from his lip. His partner gave him matches. The black guy lit his cigarette himself and threw the match down on the man. After he took two puffs he whacked the guy again. "What about that, motherfucka?" the man turned and asked Rossi.

They were on their way to putting the finishing touches on their punching bag, all the while calling Rossi a nosey-ass bitch. The white man pulled the beaten man up by his arms and held him, making him an exposed punching bag for his partner. He went Thomas Hearns on the defenseless man.

Rossi had opened his car door by now and used the door as a leaning post. He was glad that he left the last shot of cognac at the bar. "Looks like he's had enough. Why don't you guys give him a break?" Rossi damn near slurred.

When they heard Rossi's words the larger man released the arms of the man. They watched him fall to
the ground and they both turned to look at Rossi. Without even speaking they began to walk toward him.
"Look, I don't want any trouble," Rossi said.
"Too got-damn late," the smaller of the two said.
"Tonight is just not your night," the other proclaimed.
Seeing that they continued to walk toward him Rossi
bent down into his car and pulled out his pistol. Without warning he shot one in the leg and the other in the
shoulder. "Like I said, enough," Rossi repeated. Then
he checked around to make sure no one saw what he
did.
"Motherfucka shot me!" the little black one shouted.
"Oh shit, I'm shot!" he called out. The echo he created
in the garage seemed to relay three or four times. He
started limping away as fast as he possibly could so
Rossi couldn't cap him again.
The white guy holding his shoulder saw the blood
oozing from his body and started to cry. By now it was
dripping through his hand down to the ground. "Son
of a bitch," he said. "You fuckin' son of a bitch," he repeated, trying to deal with the pain.
"C'mon, this way to the car," the black guy yelled to
his partner. "Take me to the hospital!"
Using his bloody hand the white guy pointed in the
other direction, "No, it's this way, got-damn it!"
Rossi watched them limp away, licking their wounds,
trying to figure out the way to their car. He placed his
gun back in the car. Rossi glanced over at the man who
took the beating. He was pretty sure that he would be
okay when he noticed the man struggling to stand.
When Rossi proceeded to get in his car to finally go
home, he stopped cold when he heard the man say,
"Thanks, Rossi."

Chapter 50

It was early in the morning—way too early—but I had no other choice than to listen to the shocking news that was being told to me. Ely had been murdered. Beaten to a pulp and left to die in his kennel. His face was so unrecognizable that when Joyce walked out to the kennel to see what was keeping him, she could barely recognize him.

Tavious along with Saadia knocked on my door with the news. Saadia found out about the murder first. She overheard it on her police scanner that she used to keep a step ahead of other reporters on the beat. When she called Tavious he didn't believe that Ely was dead and wanted to ride out to Henry County to see what was going on for himself. Saadia was able to talk him over to my place so we could figure out what the best plan of action would be for Tavious, because by this time the police probably knew everyone Ely had been in contact with over the past few hours. That wasn't good because it put Tavious at the murder scene when he went out back to get the key to unlock Saadia from the bathroom. Tavious was in deep now. If they couldn't pin him down in Amara's case they damn sure had a better chance with Ely. Without a doubt we all knew he went out to the kennel for the key and I wanted to find out every detail about what happened, so I asked.

"Just like I said, West. I went out back to get the key and he put the dog on me before he gave me the key to unlock the door for Saadia." Tavious took a shot of whiskey and was very used to it by now.

"And after that?" I asked. Saadia was standing next to him, rubbing his shoulders.

"I already told you, man." Tavious was already pouring another drink and looked at me hard.

"Tell me again," I asked.

Tavious put the bottle down then looked at me then Saadia.

Saadia pushed, "Go ahead, baby, you don't have anything to hide."

Tavious exhaled then scanned us again before he spoke. "Ely put the dog in the cage, okay? And when he came back I pushed him. I told him he had made a mistake by putting that dog on me."

"Just a shove?" I only asked because I wanted to be clear, not because I didn't believe him.

"That's it, West. I could see the fear in his eyes. I was mad, man, but I didn't kill 'im. I just snatched the key from him and came back to the house."

Saadia was still relieving stress in his shoulders and moved forward just enough to look him in the eyes. "Was there anyone else in the kennel?"

"I don't think so. I'm pretty sure there wasn't—as crazy as that dog was he would have found them. That dog was a real medieval son'bitch. "

We went around and around close to an hour trying to figure out what the right path for Tavious would be. Tavious wanted to go back out to the house or even to the police and clear his name as soon as possible. I knew ultimately it was his decision, but if he did, there were a few things I didn't want him to mention: shoving Ely, or the dog incident. That alone would have given him motive, and with his record he'd be locked back up for sure.

"And don't tell them about the money either," Saadia said.

I gave Tavious a look of "how in the hell does she know?" when Saadia mentioned the money.

His hands turn upside down toward the ceiling. "I told her, man. I mean it's long gone so it's not even an issue anymore—right?"

For the first time I truly believed 100 percent that he was whipped and the revelation almost made me grab the bottle for a little snort.

Out of the blue my doorbell rang.

Tavious looked at his watch; it was a little past five in the morning. "Too damn early for Jehovah's Witnesses," he said. "That's gotta be the police."

I looked out my window to see who it was. There was no movement on the street, but I saw a man on the porch, looking out toward the street with his back toward my front door. It was Rossi.

Chapter 51

At first gance at Rossi no one could tell me he hadn't been drinking. The telltale signs were all in his speech, walk, and sloppy appearance. I had been able to keep the house at a low volume with Tavious and Saadia inside at such an early hour, but all bets were off when Rossi halfway stumbled inside. He took center stage, all the while, in a matter of seconds, accomplishing something I was trying not to do: wake Lauren.

When Lauren heard Rossi's loud voice as he greeted us, she came down into the room we were in, rubbing her eyes and gathering her robe all at the same time.

"Did . . . I . . . wake . . . you . . . L-boogie . . . ?" Rossi whined and teased.

No one had to tell her he'd had a few. His eyes said it all. His smile a little more. Lauren got her bearings, looked around, and noticed the whole room of guests. She did a double take on Saadia because she was sitting on Tavious's lap, kissing his face, telling him everything was going to be okay.

Saadia picked up on Lauren's attention. "Hi, again."

"Hey . . ." Lauren sang back.

Tavious found a way from her kisses and smiled at Lauren. He points to Saadia. "My lover."

"Aww geez," Rossi mumbled; then he leaned up against the wall. "We know . . . we know."

"West, what's going on?" Lauren made her way over to me and I began to fill her in.

"Well, Tavious and Saadia came over because Tavious's mother's husband Ely has been murdered." Rossi and Lauren comment at the same time. They wonder what happened and when. After I tell them I continue. "And we are trying to figure out the best way for Tavious to approach it since, after all, he could be the last person to see him alive."

I could see Lauren giving Tavious the once-over. She was like everyone else, wanting to know how the man ended up dead.

"I didn't kill him . . . I swear," Tavious said.

"Well what happened?" Lauren asked.

"They found him beaten to death," Saadia said.

"And you know this how?"

"I heard it on my police scanner," she said. "I'm a reporter."

"Right. Well, if Tavious didn't do it, then he can go to the police and let them know."

"I do that and I'm locked up for sure on my record alone. No can do, I'm not going back to jail. I need a place to lay my head."

"You can stay with me, babe," Saadia suggested, right before she kissed him on the cheek. There was a pause while the two whispered sweet somethings.

Lauren changed the loving mood and turned to Rossi. "And what's your problem?"

Rossi waited a few beats before he spoke. "I just shot two guys in a parking lot."

Chapter 52

Before Rossi could say another word I ushered him out the front door so we could talk. There was no way I was going to let him incriminate himself in front of the front-page reporter who was always looking for another story. He would always be family to me.

I tapped him on the shoulder first to get his full attention. "What the fuck, Rossi? You shot two guys in a parking lot?"

"Yep, two mopes with loud mouths," he mumbled. "West, I'm getting sleepy, man."

"Look, Rossi, just tell me what happened and I'll take you back inside and find you someplace to get some rest. This is serious, man—you understand?" I watched him try to get himself together.

"Well, you know Rita has been on my ass about my last couple of losses playing cards," he said.

"That bad, huh?"

"Well, I had another bad night, West—bad."

"Rossi, have you been drinking all night?"

"Nah, had a few at the card game and a few more after I shot the guys, that's it."

"Okay, okay, talk to me about shooting the mopes. What the hell happened?"

"Oh yeah, the mopes. Well, after my card game, I was walking out to my car and saw these fuckin' rough riders beating a guy senseless."

"Right in the parking lot?"

"Umm . . . hmm, a few feet from my car. I asked them to stop because he looked like he had enough. But I guess they didn't like me in their business and as I was getting in the car, they came over to me."

"And you shot 'em?"

Rossi stood, affirming with a head shake but looking into space as to remember. "Had to, West. I'm to fuckin' old to try the Ali shuffle."

"Kill 'em?"

Rossi pointed at himself to explain. "Naah, one in the shoulder here, the other the leg, 'bout here. They ran off after and it was over. Happened in a few seconds, man. They don't know me but I sure do know them," he said.

"How's that?"

"After I shot them, as I was getting into my car, the poor bastard who took the Mike Tyson beating called out my name."

"He fuckin' knew who you were?"

"Exactly how I felt. He called out my name and thanked me for saving his ass."

"Well, who is this guy?"

"Police."

"Police?"

"Yep, police. He was with the crew who busted up your place. He was outside on lookout. He told me they kept him outside because they don't trust him anymore."

"Trust him how? What the fuck, Rossi? What are we talking about here?"

"We went for a drink afterward. Someplace where he could get some ice for his face, you know, lick his wounds. He told me he was in this Smoke Dog unit who've been doing some really bad shit around the city."

"Yeah? I read about those idiots in the paper. So, that's the crew who tore up my place?"

Rossi nodded yes. "They're into it all, West. Drugs, guns, murder. These assholes have no regret."

"So, what was the beat down about?"

"Internal affairs."

"Say what?"

"The unit shot up an old man's house. Told everyone it was a dope house when the smoke cleared. They shot him dead and tried to plant weapons in his house when all along they had been storing drugs there for some big-name gang. Internal affairs got involved, started asking questions, and when they asked Ganes—"

"His name is Ganes?"

"Yeah, Samuel Ganes. When he was questioned he was the main reason their story began to turn sour because his explanation of what happened that night was one hundred and eighty degrees different from what the rest of the unit testified."

"So they beat his ass . . ."

"Yeah, said they had planned to kill him."

"Bunch of fuckin' crooks, man."

"That's not it, West," Rossi said.

"What more could there be?"

"Ganes was tightlipped about this. But he told me, he's pretty sure he knows who has the missing two million dollars, along with who did the murder of our girl Amara."

Chapter 53

Before Rossi could spit out anything else, Tavious rushed outside with Saadia in tow. His mother called to let him know the police were at her house and they wanted to speak with him immediately.

"He should go with me," Saadia recommended.

"I don't think that's a good idea," I let her know. I figured they would be coming to pay her a visit as well. I was somewhat sure Joyce didn't show her any love when she was questioned by the police. But Tavious was his own man. I asked him what he thought about it.

"He's right," he told Saadia.

Saadia looked up at Tavious and wrapped her arm around him then looked at me. "Well, what is he going to do?"

Tavious appeared like he wanted to run. "Fuck this, I gotta get out of here. I'm not going back to prison," Tavious promised. He looked up and down the street, paranoid.

I tried to put myself in his situation. I couldn't decide if I would go into flight mode if I was wanted for questioning for murder if innocent. His past in prison was something I couldn't even comprehend. The smell, the food, the treatment, the isolation was all too much to process.

"Look, let's just get in a car and get out of here." They were in agreement. "Sorry, Saadia, this is a boys-only outing," I had to let her know.

Saadia shrieked, "What about me?"

Tavious had to tell Saadia at least three times to go home. I went inside and let Lauren know we were on the move. She decided to call Rita and give a heads-up on Rossi. We all loaded up in Rossi's car. I made my disdain known for having to drive his BMW while he sat on the passenger side trying to catch some shut-eye. Tavious sat in the back and every time I glanced in the rearview mirror he had slid down an inch or two farther into the back seat, even though Rossi had triple black tint.

Tavious hadn't decided where he was going to lay his head for a few days so my first stop was to the apartment above the shop. I gave him three minutes to get everything he thought he would need. He was out in two. There was no sign of the police anywhere around the shop. All I noticed were three early-morning drop-offs sitting in the parking lot for service.

We still had a few hours before the shop would open up for business and I passed at least ten Waffle House establishments before I finally settled on one so we could talk. It was on the interstate going south on the route to Macon. Rossi ordered an entire pot of coffee.

"Okay, Rossi, are you ready to talk about the two million dollars?" I asked.

Tavious glanced puzzled. "two million? What're you talking about?"

"Rossi told me he may have talked to a connection to your missing money. I didn't want to tell you in front of Saadia."

"How many times do I have to tell you we can trust her?"

"Don't matter, we don't," Rossi pushed out.

I watched Rossi pour some coffee. He placed a heap of sugar in his cup and put it down, nonstop. Then he refilled and took that one halfway. "Look, like I was telling you earlier, I shot two assholes last night."

"For what?" Tavious didn't know and he was noticeably on edge knowing the police wanted to speak with him.

Rossi put up his hand and waived his question off. "Don't even matter anymore. I helped a guy out of a jam. He just happened to be one of the officers who busted up West's place."

Tavious was very interested and took the pot of coffee and poured some into his cup: black no sugar.

"Come to find out this guy is police in a special major crimes unit. The major of his unit—a hard-charging female, no-nonsense, fresh out of bubblegum type—all of a sudden put in papers for retirement."

"Shit, so what? People making moves every day," Tavious said.

"That's the point," Rossi said. "Seems to be, by all accounts, that his boss, this major, has only two years left for a full pension. So, who does that?"

"So someone walking off in the sunset gives us a tip on the two mil?" Tavious tried to understand.

"Yeah, when this major just summons a night shift into Amara's house, stealth-like—and when they get there, she's dead."

We watch Rossi refill his coffee and load it up again. This time he added cream.

"So they are instructed to go through the house, remove any pictures with Amara and the major. Then this guy Ganes specifically is told where to find a duffle bag in the stairwell of the house. He was given specific instructions to meet the major the same night in the same parking lot where I see these two mopes knocking him around."

"Wait a minute—if the police found her body, why was it still there when I went to see Amara?"

"They were told to leave the body, so they did. Ganes said he and the others figured their major was setting someone up. Look, man, these guys, this unit, did bogus raids, arrests, and drug rips. They are ruthless and don't give a fuck who they do."

"They knew you were getting out, Tavious," I let him know. "You were the only person to know about the money other than Amara. They wanted to silence you and have a reason to lock you back up."

Tavious thought for a moment and things clicked. "And Ely knew."

"And he's dead," I reminded him.

"But how?"

"Who knows?"

"So now we know who has the money?" Tavious questioned.

"Maybe," Rossi confirmed, as he took in more coffee.

Chapter 54

It was clear to us that the major crimes unit and their fearless leader knew all about Tavious. They'd been trying to set him up all along. It felt good that we knew where all of this was coming from now. But it was very frustrating to know we were once again going to battle with some ruthless Atlanta police who were taking orders and carrying them out without any hesitation for a higher-ranking official who couldn't care less about anything except getting paid.

First things were first. Tavious needed to go underground and make himself ghost until we somehow cleared his name. Something inside of me wanted him to go to the police—maybe to someone Mrs. Bullock trusted. He could turn himself in and go face to face with anyone who had questions. But when I mentioned it he didn't want any part of stepping back into any place that had bars attached.

Tavious did agree that we should at least pull his Grand's coattail. I couldn't go another step further without letting Mrs. Bullock know what had transpired. When we got her on the phone it was no surprise that she already had some insight. She had talked with Joyce, who was hysterical and having a bad time coming to grips that Ely was dead. Mrs. Bullock told Tavious that his mother didn't want to think he killed Ely. But she wanted Tavious to tell her so out of his own mouth. He did. Then Joyce told Tavious she stopped answering police questions when she realized that after the police from the APD found out Tavious had been on the property, they were coaxing Henry County police to claim it was Tavious who did the deed. Mrs. Bullock gave all the wisdom she had to Tavious. She let him know maybe the best thing for him to do was to turn himself in before they even got around to issuing a warrant for his arrest. But he wasn't hearing it, even when I put my two cents in one last time to agree with her.

Without any hesitation after agreeing with us that Tavious needed to lay low, Mrs. Bullock gave us a residential address in the city of Decatur. She asked us to take Tavious there because she said he would be safe.

On the way out to Decatur there was not much to say. Almost felt like we were in a losing battle. One thing for sure, we were going up against authorities that required a clear explanation and evidence for freedom. Tavious knew he had to leave this entire situation up to us if he ever was going to get up from underneath the smell of this bad situation. There was nothing he could do about it except stay out of the way and hope for the best.

When we stopped at a red light, I heard the hammer on a pistol lock. I looked back at Tavious; he gazed into my eyes, nodding his head up and down. Then he put the piece back into his backpack. He told me Saadia gave it to him before she left. It was her protection when she went into the hood for a story. Now for the first time he was breaking the law. He had to know if he was caught with the piece it was another mandatory sentence. I wanted to remind him of the fact. But no doubt about it—he knew.

We arrived at the address Mrs. Bullock gave to us. It was in a quiet neighborhood not far from Emory University. Rossi got out the car and knocked on the door of the flat-level, all-brick house. No answer. He put his hand down into the gold vase that sat on the right side of the door just like Mrs. Bullock instructed. The key was inside. He unlocked the door and waved us in. I waited for Tavious to go in; then I followed him a couple of minutes later just to be sure we wouldn't call attention.

I walked in and couldn't help but notice how up to date the house was. It was very clean inside. There were two bedrooms and one bathroom, as it was an older house, but there was no doubt it would serve the purpose of keeping Tavious safe. While we all looked around Tavious took out a CD Saadia gave to him. He turned on the system sitting in the living room and the first song that blared through the speakers was "Strawberry Letter 23" by The Brothers Johnson. We all took just a few seconds and smiled. When Tavious opened the fridge and noticed it was stacked with food for at least two weeks it became obvious that Mrs. Bullock knew he would need someplace to stay. It sealed the deal when Tavious found the case of brews sitting on top of the fridge. All we had to do now was pay our new major friend a visit and get to the bottom of things, because there was one thing we all agreed upon: that soon enough the police would have an All Points Bulletin to bring Tavious in, or worse.

Chapter 55

About an hour after we left Tavious, Mrs. Bullock called to ensure things were okay. I found out the house was one of many rentals that she had. It would be almost impossible for anyone to connect it to her and Tavious. It was under her deceased husband's name and a fifty-year-old LLC. I could feel the urgency in her voice.

"West, you know time is our enemy now," she started.

I agreed and continued to listen into the phone.

"I think it's time for us to take advantage of this connection to the reporter of the *AJC*."

"What do you mean?"

"She has an audience, West. She has a column that is highly respected and we can use her notoriety to help us. Help us get the word out about these crooked cops and all their shenanigans. We don't want her to use Tavious's name in any of this. But we need her to draw attention to the police connections to these murders and Ely's connection to the department by supplying them with those trained dogs. Maybe this will slow them down."

I fully understood what Mrs. Bullock was saying. The police were knee-deep in this for sure. If we could get Saadia to print such that would give us extra time to connect the dots to the murders. It would help with the perceived evidence the police had on Tavious.

It was late, but we couldn't wait until morning to call Saadia to get her on board with our plan. The way she felt about Tavious no doubt was going to work in our favor. I called Tavious to get her number and explain to her what we needed. He wanted to call Saadia himself. But Rossi didn't think he should. Saadia was crafty. Their relationship was hot like fire. If Tavious heard her voice and they connected it would be the end of his secret hiding place. After going back and forth with Tavious he finally agreed.

It was almost two in the morning when I dialed her number. The phone didn't finish the first ring before she picked up.

"Tavious?"

"Saadia, it's West."

"West? What's wrong? Is Tavious okay?"

"Yes, he's fine."

"Where is he?"

"He's fine," I repeated.

After I was sure she knew I was not giving anything up on Tavious, I hit her up with our request. "Tavious needs a favor," I told her.

"Anything, what is it?"

"The police are going to do him, Saadia. They are going to charge him with the murders of Ely and Amara and we've connected the police to the murders but can't prove it."

"The police?"

"That's right."

"And I can help how?"

"I have some information for you and we need you to print it in that newspaper of yours."

"And this information is concerning . . . ?"

I wasn't sure, but it seemed Saadia picked up a pen and a pad that reporters keep at the ready.

"APD's major crimes unit," I told her.

"Really now?"

I was sure she sat up in the bed when she heard what I said.

"A Major Curruth and her corrupt unit, you familiar?"

Saadia was very receptive to the information I had for her. I relayed the info we had gotten through Rossi's police informant. At the end of our conversation she was sure that she could do the article about the wrongdoings of the unit. She told me it would include Amara's murder and the ransacking of her place, along with the possible connection to Ely and his K-9s he provided to the police department.

At the end of the conversation Saadia wanted to meet the informant. Saadia said there was no way she could print so many damning allegations without sitting down and looking into the informant's eyes herself. Secondhand from me was not good enough.

Chapter 56

I was able to get a few hours sleep after my phone conversation with Saadia. When I woke up Lauren wasn't shy about making her feelings known. She knew that I was busy, but she missed me and wanted to spend some time together. I understood how she felt because we were so into our lives before Tavious and the two million along with the murders. I declared to my sweetheart that I missed her too. So much that I wanted to take her out.

"We're going to a funeral?" were her first words when I pulled up into the funeral parlor out in the Cascades. "West, you're taking me to a freakin' funeral as a date?" she shrieked.

I hadn't completely parked the car yet, but I still answered her. "Yes, babe, real quick though. I need to check something out. Won't be but a minute."

"West, when you told me we were going out, I thought at the very least some Smokin' Bones and a nice afternoon drink, then back home for some loving. But a freakin' funeral? You are now on top of my hot-mess list."

"I couldn't tell you, Lauren. If I did, you wouldn't have come—am I right?"

"Right. You know you're right."

"And that's why I didn't. Please, just go in for a second and we'll be out. We'll go anyplace you want."

I had taken the keys out the ignition and looked at a few people walk inside the funeral home before Lauren even answered.

"So, whose friggin' funeral is this anyway?"

"Ely's," I told her. "Poor bastard got beat to death in his own place of business. All those got-damn dogs he had and not one could save his ass. He was Tavious's mother's husband."

"Well, I tell you what, if you don't take me out as soon as we leave this place, there is going to be another funeral. C'mon, let's go."

I tried to kiss Lauren on the cheek but she pushed the car door open and was ready to get our visit over with. When we get inside there was no hiding the fact that the easily identifiable police were there, wearing out-of-style street clothing and checking out every last person who entered.

Inside I see Joyce and Mrs. Bullock talking, while about twenty or so others stood chatting. I took Lauren by the hand to make our way over to the ladies and overheard two men speaking about all the dogs Ely was leaving behind. They were wondering if it would be a good time to approach Joyce about purchasing them.

After I introduced Joyce to Lauren she and Mrs. Bullock thanked us for coming. I couldn't believe that something so awful could have happened so quickly and without anyone noticing anything. I didn't want to get Joyce's hopes up too high and divulge any information that we were looking into. But I did need to find out from her if Ely had been in any kind of disagreement with anyone he was doing business with on the police force.

"No, I'm not familiar with anyone from a major crimes unit," Joyce said.

I didn't want to but I pushed her some more and asked her again.

"Wait a minute," she said. "One night, I remember Ely getting a call from the police, and they wanted him to bring out Max."

"Max?"

"Yes, that's one of Ely's prime dogs. The police wanted Ely to bring her to some kind of raid or something and wanted the dog to sniff something out or something like that."

"So, they were looking for something?"

"I can't say, but I do know that he took the dog out and came back early in the morning."

Mrs. Bullock could tell Joyce was close to another breaking point. She asked Lauren if she would take her down to the first row to sit down and we watched them walk away.

"Poor girl," Mrs. Bullock said. "His death has her feeling like she's lost her entire world."

"I'm sure she's dealing with a lot," I let her know.

"West, I noticed all these police officers here, so I won't say too much."

I just nodded my head and looked at a few of the officers who had made themselves at home. One in particular who was an uninvited guest to my home couldn't keep his eyes off me.

"Did everything work out with our friend?"

I took Mrs. Bullock by the arm and began to walk with her down the aisle to her seat next to Joyce. "We're going to sit down as soon as possible, and when that happens, I'll let you know."

She made me promise to do just that.

Chapter 57

I swear my intentions were to spend quality time with Lauren while we sat and ate an early dinner at her favorite rib joint. And we were doing just that. While enjoying our meal, I had just mentioned to Lauren what a wise choice she made in our dinner spot. I was seriously thinking about ordering another stack of ribs and a drink. That was until Rossi called. He let me know that he was with his contact. This guy was adamant about not sitting down with Saadia to share what he knew about the major crimes unit. Lauren picked up on my uneasiness. When the waiter came to check on us she asked for a takeout box and told me to go handle my business.

Lauren didn't say much when I pulled into our driveway, other than I could get in by myself; then she opened the door and walked off. I thought about going after her but there was no use. Our date had been ruined.

I picked Rossi up in about twenty minutes.

"We're going to do what?" Rossi wanted to know.

"Going to go back over your boy's, take him over Saadia's so she can do that got-damn article," I told him.

Rossi gave me the directions to his home as we drove. He damn sure didn't have a problem with what I wanted to do. The only thing I remember Rossi saying was something or other about getting his cut of the money so he could put it in the bank. He needed to get a handle on his gambling.

During the drive we called Tavious and revealed what was happening. Tavious gave us Saadia's address. He was anxious to hear some results of what we had going because he needed some relief from the mounting pressure he was feeling. I told him we would let him know as soon as we could, if not sooner.

Chapter 58

We made it to Samuel Ganes's home. We knocked. He finally answered.

"Sammy, baby," Rossi said.

Ganes had his door open about half an inch. I could see half his eye. "Rossi? What the fuck? I already told you—not doing it."

"Now, now, Sammy," Rossi eased.

"Who the fuck is he?"

Ganes had his eye on me, and through that little-ass crack in the door, I could tell the police had really whooped his ass in that parking garage.

"He's my guy," Rossi let him know. "His name is West. I've told you all about him."

"Why'd you bring him here?"

Rossi changed his weight on his stance from left to right. "Don't, Sammy, you know why."

"Can't do it," Sammy decided. He tried to slam the door.

At exactly the same time Rossi and I put our hands up to the door and pushed it backward. He fell to the ground.

Rossi looked down at him. "Shit, man, you have no strength left after that ass beating, do you?"

Right after Ganes picked himself up from the floor, he told us he was getting ready to work the night shift. He was paranoid about us being there and said he had an eerie feeling someone was watching his every mood.

He wanted us out of his house with the quickness. But we refused to leave. It was time for desperate measures. Over and over again we made it clear that Saadia wouldn't print his name or give him up. Ganes didn't want to hear what we were selling and told us to go fuck ourselves. He reinforced that we had no idea who we were dealing with and he wished he'd never told Rossi anything at all.

I didn't want to hear Ganes's bullshit. It was too late for the Monday-morning quarterbacking that he was spewing. I told him that if he wanted to play the game like that I would just give his name to the reporter and tell her to use it as she pleased.

Five minutes later he was dressed for his night shift and sitting in the back seat of my car on his way with us to see Saadia.

When we knocked on Saadia's door she took one look at our officer in uniform and quickly ushered us inside.

"You brought a fully dressed cop to my house?"

We all stood in the foyer waiting for her to guide us in. She shut the door and Ganes went back to the door and pulled the curtain back on the pane to see if anyone had followed us.

"Are you sure you guys want to keep this a secret?" Saadia took a good look at Ganes. "Never in my life have I had a cop in full uniform about to spill the beans on some corruption."

"Had to bring him as is," I let her know. "He starts his shift in forty-five minutes so we need to do this," I clarified.

Saadia led us into her sitting room, which was right off of the front door. It was a sunken living room. When we all were seated she looked at Ganes. "You have some information for me?"

Chapter 59

The deed for the article was done. Saadia seemed to be content with the information Ganes gave to her. I paid close attention as she asked questions that only a seasoned reporter could, to confirm what she was being told. When she felt she had enough, she quickly ushered us to the door so that Ganes could get to work. She declared she would have something for the paper in the morning as long as her editor approved it, which she didn't think would be a problem.

It was already late, and after we dropped Ganes off at his place there was nothing else to do other than go to the address we had for the major. It was time to try to find out if our hunch was right that the two million was stashed someplace in the house.

We parked the car close to the house and sat for a while. We were only a few houses down from the driveway. The house was dark with no movement inside.

Rossi rolled down his window and looked over at the house. "Just like old times, partner."

"Just like," I agreed.

"I say we go in," Rossi decided.

"No one in sight and the fact they burst into people's places anytime they want, that alone gives me enough motivation to check it out."

"You think that money is inside—don't you?"

"Yeah, I do, this major is playing everyone. Keeping this quiet little place. What is this, a one-, two-bedroom flat? One garage? The only other option is to have this place surrounded by police cars twenty-four-seven, keeping an eye out for the money, and that's too loud, man. People would suspect something."

I wasn't sure if the money was inside, but the only way we were going to find out was to go inside and check for ourselves. One thing we both were sure of was that the major definitely had an alarm system on the house. I sat in the car while Rossi went to the back-yard to find the electrical box connection to cut the system off. It took Rossi only a few minutes to finish the job. We decided to go to a nearby Walmart to pick up another flashlight with batteries. When we returned there was still no movement or lights on in the house. We waited another thirty minutes before we made our move to go inside.

Chapter 60

Rossi noticed a glass sliding door when he was disconnecting the alarm. We made it our point of entry. Of course it didn't take him long to get the door open. He pried the screen open with a screwdriver and used the same tool by unscrewing two screws connected to the lock on the door. We watched the entire lock mechanism fall to the ground as Rossi called it some cheap-ass shit.

It didn't take long to get our bearings and finally see the layout of the house. When we stepped in we were right between the kitchen and what looked to be a sitting room that had an HD TV mounted on the wall. We didn't know what kind of time we were working with to search for the money so I pointed for Rossi to go one way and I was in the wind in another.

I pointed my flashlight toward the kitchen and stood for a few seconds wondering where to start. I noticed that there were quite a few cabinets and drawers. Some were over a built-in desk with a computer sitting on top. That's where I started my search. I pushed the Enter key on the keyboard but it had no power so I reached down to the computer and turned it on. While I waited I opened up the two cabinet doors above the desk. With the help of my flashlight, I could see two shelves. One of the shelves was half full with books that were lined up in an orderly fashion. Most had something or other to do with police tactics and urban

security. The other shelves where filled with all types
of other knick-knacks: deck of cards, light bulbs, an
old Rolodex, and a small camcorder and so much other
shit that I just got tired of looking at it. I took my arm
and started to throw it all to the floor searching for the
money. I noticed the computer came on but I decided
to unplug it. I took it along with the camcorder and
placed it near the door so I could take it back to see if
Rita and Lauren could find anything on it.

We were in and out the house searching for the
money in about forty-five minutes and, sad to say, no
money was in sight. The one thing we did find out was
that the major didn't seem to spend much time in her
residence of record, which Rossi's snitch copied off
their emergency contact list. We came to that conclu-
sion because once we started searching through the
house it was in perfect order. It didn't seem to have
someone there on a day-to-day basis. There were no
towels in the bathroom, no dishes in the sink, and no
clothes in the washer or dryer.

It rained all the way back to my place. When we
went inside Lauren and Rita were sitting in front of
the television, snacking on popcorn and drinks while
watching a show Lauren had recorded sometime ago,
called *Single Ladies*. They hardly noticed that we were
dripping wet when we walked through the door. It almost felt like they shooed us into the kitchen while they
giggled and laughed about the show. At least Lauren
was smiling.

I put the computer we took from the major's house
along with the camcorder on the counter, and retrieved
a few beers from the fridge, then handed one to Rossi.

"I can't believe it, not a damn thing to be found in
that house," I said.

"This major is crafty, man—maybe more so than we ever thought. I mean it was a nice try but I would probably keep two million dollars so close that you would think I was making love to it," Rossi admitted.

"You're probably right. That money is so close that we are going to have to get an eyeball on this major and just follow her until it's revealed."

"You talking twenty-four-hour surveillance?"

"Maybe . . ."

Rossi's immediate expression was not pleasant.

"No other way around it."

Rossi thought for a minute. "I never thought it was going to be this difficult. I mean it's not like I've ever tried to help a man get his two million dollars of drug money back that sat in the wall of a friend for twenty years and is now connected to multiple murders and police. But geez, man, who are we dealing with here?"

I didn't get a chance to answer Rossi because the ladies entered the kitchen. There was no hiding that it was not soda in their glasses.

"Wow, what a crazy show!" Lauren said in her outside voice. She kissed me on the cheek and then put her glass down on the table.

Rita was close behind. "You got that right. Hey, Rossi, would you ever cheat on me?"

Rossi was taken aback by Rita's question because her conversation was 180 degrees from what was on his mind. "Rita, are you serious?" he wanted to know.

"Of course I am. I didn't even know people in Atlanta were so shady. There are so many places to go and do the nasty without getting caught."

Rossi didn't say a word. The look on his face gave Rita all that was on his mind.

"Okay, okay, yes . . . it's no secret about my past life. But geez, I didn't think everyone was doing it—and for free." She chuckled.

"It was a television show you were watching," I reminded her.

It didn't take Lauren long to focus on the computer. They were so busy watching their show when we walked in she hadn't even noticed.

"So, what's this?"

"Computer and a camcorder," I let her know.

"Okay . . ." she sang.

"We're going to sit here and go through it and see if there's anything that can help us with Tavious."

"Where is he by the way?" Lauren wanted to know.

"Oh, he's fine," Rossi interrupted.

"I didn't ask that," Lauren said.

I could tell Rossi and Lauren were close to getting into one of their loving squabbles so I went in quick. "So, will you ladies help to see what's on this computer for us?"

"Sorry, babe," Lauren said. "I'm on my way to bed. I was caught up knee-deep in getting your receipts in order on your desk all day and I'm beat."

"That makes two of us, honey," Rita decided. "This drink has a sister wanting her pillow." Rita kissed Laruen on the cheek, then told Rossi to take her home so they could continue their conversation in the car.

Rossi looked at me and shook his head back and forth.

"I'll take the computer, man," Rossi told me. "I'll have her check it out in the morning," he confirmed.

Chapter 61

Not getting much sleep had programmed my body to do just that. My self-mandated requirement of eight hours' sleep had become a thing of the past since we were on the hunt for the money. I'd curled up into the bed next to Lauren until about three in the morning, when my tossing and turning wouldn't allow me to sleep any longer. My intentions were to make coffee and fiddle around with the camcorder we took from the major's. But there was no coffee so I quietly went out the house to the grocery store to buy some so the coffee wouldn't be an issue once Lauren was up for the day.

To my surprise the store had way more people than I expected. The twenty-minute wait I had to endure with the two shoppers in front of me with baskets full of items didn't help matters. After the cashier swore to me she would have let me move in front of her if she had been the customer in front of me and noticed that I only had a can of Chock full o'Nuts coffee and her basket was full with almost $200 of groceries, I noticed the *AJC* delivery man slam a stack of morning papers on the counter. I picked one up and asked the cashier to add it to my bill.

"Dang, you already doin' coffee and it's barely five in the morning," Lauren said from behind me as she stood in her T-shirt with her hands on her hips.

"Couldn't sleep, babe, so I went out and got some when I realized we didn't have any."

"Pour me some when it's ready?"

Lauren moved toward the kitchen table and asked if I'd seen her house shoes, then took a seat at the table. I grabbed some cups from the cabinet and placed them on the table. I noticed the coffee was just about ready so I stood in front of the maker waiting for the last drop to fall through, while I told Lauren about the lady shopper in the store with all the groceries and how I would have let her move in front of me if I would have had an army-load of food to check out. As I continued to give my two cents about the lady and the lack of human decency people display, Lauren gave me the customary early morning acknowledgment of a nod and a yawn. The coffee was ready. I picked up the pot, went to the table, poured it into our cups, then went into the fridge for the hazelnut cream. She still hadn't responded to what I said to her about the lady in front of me at the store. I could see some of the major headlines on the front page about the Atlanta school system and the cheating by principals and teachers that had occurred resulting from the No Child Left Behind Act.

"Wow, that paper really must be interesting," I said to her. I sat down at the table and took a sip of my coffee. "So, are they throwing all the teachers and principals in jail? Hey, maybe the prisons can save a bit on contractors teaching coming in with their own on site," I said to her.

Lauren looked up at me. I'd known her way too long not to tell something wasn't right. She didn't say what was wrong; she just slid the entire newspaper toward me and started on her own coffee and told me to relax.

After my turn at reading the paper it was as though I'd been smacked in the face. I couldn't believe it. Saadia had thrown Tavious under the bus in a scathing article that just about implicated him in the killings of

Amara and Ely. Her article was a local news front-page story; and not only had she written her accounts on how she thought the murders occurred, but she added a dark picture of Tavious that made him look murderous and hardened. Her call for a manhunt by the APD to find him and throw away the key was enough to send me quickly over the edge.

I threw the paper on the table and asked Lauren to get my cell phone. I wanted to talk to Saadia pronto, but, as I expected, when I called there was no answer. The article that I had just finished reading was 180 degrees from what we had discussed with her. There was no mention of the police major crime unit or any of the unlawful bullshit they had been doing passing it off as police work.

The audacity of Saadia calling her article her best work ever. She applauded herself for going undercover to find out more about Tavious after her contacts told her he was initially under investigation for the murder of Amara. She even went so far as to write about spending a day with his mother and now understanding where his anger came from. Saadia was not shy about letting everyone know that Tavious was the last person to ever see Ely alive. She wrote that he was fresh out of prison after twenty years and the prison system had hardened him. Her article said that when he got home to retrieve money that he left with his drug mule, she had spent it all. She claimed he snapped and took her life, then weeks later took Ely's because men in his mother's life had always taken her from him and he had never been able to deal with seeing his mother hurt.

I called Rossi and briefly explained what Tavious was now up against. I took a quick shower and asked him to meet me at the spot where Tavious was staying.

Mrs. Bullock had always been an early riser. Before I even got out of the shower she had called my cell and Lauren let her know we were on our way to see Tavious. She let me know that she would be there just as soon as she could.

I didn't like the look on Lauren's face when I jumped in my car just after she called out to me and ran out to give me the camcorder and newspaper that I'd left sitting on the kitchen table. She knew that things were coming to a head.

"You're goin' to be careful—right?"

I put the car in reverse. "Yeah, yeah, it will be fine."

"I'm not worried about it, West. I'm worried about you. Promise me right now you won't put yourself in a dangerous position where you might get hurt."

I hadn't even let the fact that two people had been murdered and a shady reporter had just about told the world who was responsible for them put me in that space where I was in danger. But I had to console my baby.

"I promise you, Lauren. Promise, I will be back here soon, safe and sound." With that I let the car roll down the driveway in reverse and kept my eyes on Lauren as she gave me her kiss and customary peace sign as I drove away.

Chapter 62

I didn't get a chance to knock on the door before Tavious swung it open and snatched the paper out of my hand.

"This is bullshit, West."

"So, you heard?"

"Grands called. Got me all riled and shit." Tavious sat down to read the paper. More than likely he was reading the headline: Ex-drug Kingpin on Murderous Rampage in Atlanta. "This is bullshit! What the fuck is she thinking?"

When Tavious mentioned Saadia I pulled out my phone and called her number again. No answer.

"What the fuck did you guys talk to her about, man?"

"Just like we said," I told him. I almost felt guilty for going to see her backstabbing ass. "We told her about the connections to the raid on Amara's house and the major crimes unit along with Ely. We told her everything. It had nothing to do with you."

Tavious didn't respond; he was still reading. I sat down on the couch just knowing it was only a matter of seconds before he would explode again.

"What the fuck does she mean I have been made a hardened criminal in prison without any feeling to society? Are you kidding me!" Tavious threw the paper on the floor and stood up. "West, I don't understand this, man. Somebody needs to tell me something or I just might hurt a fool on this shit. This right here in

this paper is liable to get me the chair, man. The fuckin'
chair!"

There was a knock on the door. We knew it was Rossi
because he announced himself as he continued knocking. He came in and looked around.

"What the fuck, man?"

"You got that right," Tavious said. "They got me all
in the papers, man. Whole got-damn city is looking at
my face, thinking I'm running around killing people."

"Why would she write this mess?" Rossi said. "Did
you have it out with her or something, Tavious?"

Tavious looked at Rossi. "No. I thought we were cool.
We've only talked a few times since I've been here. She
asked to come see me, I said it wouldn't be good, and
that was that."

"We have to go see her," I decided.

"We sure as hell do," Tavious said.

Chapter 63

By the grace of God Mrs. Bullock came over a few minutes later. She was worried and tired. I hated to see her with so much stress for her grandson. So much stress about anything. Joyce was with her. They convinced Tavious to stay in the house until we could find out why Saadia printed all the lies about Tavious.

"Call her again," Rossi said. He had just gotten off the phone with Ganes, who wanted to know why the reporter served Tavious up on a royal platter. He called to tell Rossi he was getting the hell out of town. He didn't want to end up dead next behind her bullshit because there was no telling when she was going to out him.

"She has everyone in hiding," I let him know.

Rossi picked up the camcorder and turned it on as we drove. "Something seriously has to be wrong with a chick who would print a bunch of lies about someone without any cause, man. I mean freakin' serious issues."

"Just doesn't make any sense," I tell him. "Here is a woman telling this man she loves him and to do this? This is the type of shit movies are made of. Fuckin' wild and unpredictable people living for themselves. That's all it is."

Rossi didn't respond. All I heard him say was, "*Ohhh, shit*." He was looking through the camcorder viewfinder. "Oh . . . oh . . . aww . . . Just fuck me," he said.

"What?"

"Just fuck me, man," he repeated.

I slammed on the breaks. "What is it? What the hell are you talking about?"

Rossi handed me the camcorder. "Isn't this our girl?"

I focused in to find out what he was talking about. "Just fuck me too," I said.

"Yeah, that's what it looks like they're doin'," Rossi said.

"Saadia and the major?" I was speechless.

"In the flesh, brother," Rossi said.

"I'll be damned." My eyes couldn't believe what I was seeing. Saadia and the major doing things that only grown people should do. I looked at Rossi. "Saadia and the major?"

"Yup," he answered.

"Together in the bed?"

"Yup, very much so, if you ask me."

"What the hell is really going on?" I wanted to know.

When I stopped the car I didn't bother to pull over to the curb. I didn't care that the few cars that had to go around me came with a finger outside the window. To say the least after I finished watching the tape of the major and Saadia doing their dirty little deed, I put the car in drive and pushed down hard on the gas because I couldn't wait to show Ms. Thang her movie and find out what she thought about it.

There was no way I could keep our find from Tavious. When I called him the phone call wasn't about the money or who did the murders, but at least I had something positive to give to him that we were on the right track on finding out what the hell was going on. At first when I told him what we discovered on the camcorder he didn't want to believe it. For some reason he thought he would have picked up on Saadia. But that wasn't the case. Saadia had fooled us all, and we were driving down the street she lived on when we spotted her car pulling out of her driveway.

"Speed up, man, don't let her get out of that driveway," Rossi said.

I did and right before her car reached the street my car pulled up behind her and I hit the horn hard so that Saadia didn't run into my sweet baby. Her tires screeched and she jumped out the car. She called me an asshole and a few other choice words.

When she saw our faces right after we got out the car her whole demeanor changed and her eyes widened.

"So, imagine running into you today," I said. She knew damn well why we were paying her a visit.

Saadia gave me and Rossi a quick glancing over and starting walking back to her car. "Move the car or I'm calling the police," she said.

"Do you believe this shit, man?" Rossi said. We were both standing in her driveway now.

"Well, you better believe it, got-damn it," she said. "For all I know you two are killers too."

Saadia was just about in her car. I looked around as quick as I could to see if anyone was looking at me. I grabbed her car door so she couldn't get in the car. "You're not going anywhere," I told her.

She looked at my hand on the door. "Mr. West Owens, you better not do this," she said as firm as she could but I could tell she was nervous.

"Ask her if she wants to do this here or inside, West," Rossi said.

"Do what?" Saadia wanted to know.

"Ask her, West."

"We need to talk. We can do it out here or inside your house."

"There isn't a damn thing we need to talk about anyway, so you two can leave."

I kind of chuckled at her boldness. "Is that right?"

"Yes, it is," she confirmed.

"Well, that's not what the tape of you licking on the
major tells me."

We had gotten her attention. Her ears popped up
like a small puppy hearing an unfamiliar sound.

"So tell us, sweetheart, where do you want to do
this?" Rossi asked again.

We followed her into her place after we parked our
cars and she still had the nerve to have an attitude.

She put her hand on her hip. "So, what's this about?"

Rossi and I looked at each other at the same time.

"Get real," I said.

Rossi swiped at his face. "Geez. Fuckin' amnesia isn't
going to work today, believe that."

Saadia looked at our faces, knowing that she didn't
have a chance. "Okay, yeah, I wrote the article," she
pushed.

"Duh, we freakin' know that, doll," Rossi said.

"Why? What the fuck, Saadia? We didn't tell you any
of that mess you printed in that paper," I told her.

"I friggin' know that. I mean did you see a statement
of yours in quotes with your name attached?"

"No, but I saw a bunch of bullshit lies. Now I have a
friend who is worried about the rest of his life because
of the mess that showed up in the paper this morning."

We came to a point where Rossi and I were just looking at Saadia, waiting for her to tell us the deal. You
could have heard a pin drop inside for a least a minute
or so.

"Would love to stand here all day and look at you,
babe," Rossi said.

"But that's not going to happen," I let her know.

Saadia ran her hands through her hair. "Shit, he just wouldn't talk to me. I wanted to talk to him and he didn't want to talk."

"What?" I asked her.

Rossi said, "Who are we talking about?"

"Tavious, Tavious, got-damn it. He's an asshole who took advantage of me," she said.

Rossi and I glanced at each other, hoping the other knew what the hell she was talking about. She felt our confusion.

"I fell in love with him, damn it. And he pulls away from me after we had such a connection," she said.

"Now, I understand you two spent quite a bit of time together but . . . love?" I questioned.

"You have no idea. None whatsoever, West. That man told me his feelings and he gets in trouble and all of a sudden he decides that I can't know where he is. I can't see him. So, yeah, yes, I wrote the article to get him back and the shit hurts, doesn't it?"

"So, you do him because he's protecting himself?" Rossi made clear.

"And because you're hurting 'cause you can't see him? C'mon . . ." I added.

"I know, I know, I'm sorry now. I don't know what got into me. I was up all last night thinking what this was going to do to him. I just haven't had much success with men in my life, relationships period. I'm sorry; will you tell him I'm sorry, West?"

I wasn't feeling Saadia's "woe is me" concert. It would have been a hell of an act for someone else. But we didn't have time to entertain her lies. While she stood in front of us in a puddle of her tears, I held my hand out and asked Rossi to give me the camcorder.

She wiped her eyes and looked at it. "So, you want to put this on tape to show Tavious how sorry I am or something?"

Rossi looked at me, bewildered. "You believe this?"

I chuckled. "Not a chance."

"Unbelievable," Rossi mumbled.

I opened the recorder and hit the rewind button.

"Well, what's the camera for?" she wanted to know.

"You'll find out soon enough," Rossi told her.

I walked over to Saadia and pushed play on the camcorder. It ran for about three seconds.

"Where did you get that?" she screamed. It was the recording of Saadia and our mystery major conjoined and configured in a way that they seemed to enjoy.

"My, my, my," Rossi purred. "I only look at stuff like this when the little lady goes out to get her hair done. Or, on a real good night, when she's feeling a little freaky too."

"I don't think I've ever met a real-life porn star," I let her know.

Rossi asked Saadia, "Can I have your autograph?"

Chapter 64

While we sat with Saadia, Mrs. Bullock called us two times. The situation had become hot and she and Joyce were at the house with Tavious. She had already received two phone calls from police letting her know that they were headed to her house to search for Tavious. Her good standing with the APD higher-ups and city council personnel persuaded them to agree not to make a spectacle of her home front, as long as she would bring Tavious in before six in the evening; or they would be forced to put an APB out for him.

There was no time to waste and as nice as it would have been to sit down and hear about all of Saadia and the major's intimate outings and romps, we had to put the pressure on Saadia and find out everything she knew about the major to help keep Tavious from going back to prison.

I sensed Saadia was being protective of the major. The only thing she actually confided to us was that the major hated her parents for naming her Keisha Champaign Majors and was ecstatic when she made major so she could demand to be called it at all times. Saadia conceded that she had been involved with the major and they were only friends. But we weren't buying it.

"Look, it's getting close to twelve o'clock and you haven't really given us anything that we can use to get these murders off Tavious," Rossi said. He was sitting on her couch, still looking at the camcorder.

"I have a man who in six hours will turn himself in on murder charges that he didn't commit and you seem to be fine with it," I told her. "I'm just saying all this love you claim you have for Tavious and you're not being up front with us. I can tell you're holding something back. Tell me, where were you going when we pulled up behind you?"

Saadia was getting more and more agitated. "Look, yes, we have been together and for me it was just out of curiosity. I'm tired of you calling me a liar."

Rossi stood up from the couch. "Well, well, well, looky here," he said.

Rossi walked over to me and gave me the camera. In a matter of seconds my eyes were focused on the major and yet another woman having what seemed to be the time of their lives in a romantic liaison. I watched as the major and the pretty-looking, petite cutie-pie friend exchanged tender kisses, posing for the camera.

Saadia moved closer to me. I reversed the tape and pushed play so she could see. After she got her bearings and tuned in to understand what was going on, she watched the major and friend just as I had. But her reaction was tightening eyes and clear agitation. Saadia threw the camcorder down when the major said, "This must be love," and blew a kiss into the camera. That's when Saadia threw down the camcorder and screamed, "Bitch," over and over again before running out the room and down the hall of her home.

Chapter 65

The time on my cell read a quarter past two in the afternoon. We had been sitting on Saadia's couch for nearly forty-five minutes, waiting for her to come out of her room. Her crying and screaming at the walls had ended about five minutes earlier. I thought just maybe she had it all out of her system. Maybe she was ready to come out and tell us what was going on. Soon after, we could hear her talking, but not at the walls. She was having a conversation with someone. I walked down to her room, pressed my ear on her door, and realized that she was on the phone.

"Yes, yes, I know got-damn it," she said. "Do you always have to tell me about your friggin' fee when I am trying to explain something—my feelings—to you? Yes, I get it, four hundred dollars, you fuckin' tick," she said. "All I need you to do is help me with my decision. Yes, I know, I know it's the right thing and I should never do something for revenge. But got-damn it, you can dress it up all you like, but what I have for her she'll always remember."

Then for the first time in nearly an hour, Saadia's room had become completely quiet. From the outside looking in I envisioned her sitting on her bed with her face in her hands. I gave her a few more minutes before I knocked. She answered me on the fourth knock right after I called out her name.

"What is it?"

"Want to or not, Saadia— we need to talk."
No response.
"Saadia, I know that you must be feeling pretty bad.
Especially when someone has done you wrong."
"West, you don't know anything about me or how I'm
feeling, okay? So please, stop analyzing me. I just got off
the phone with my shrink. I don't need another."
I had her talking so I jumped at my chance to engage
her because time was ticking. "You're right. You're
right. I don't know you at all. The only thing I know is
that you and Tavious, although you two haven't spoken
in a few days, could really have something special."
"Yeah, but he didn't show me that he cared," she
slashed.
I paused. I really wanted to just step back and kick
her door down because I felt myself becoming quite
perturbed. Really, how could he be head over heels in
love with her in such a short time? I was furious about
the entire situation; besides, I thought she had feelings
for the major. I fought like hell to control my leg from
kicking it down, but not the tone of my voice, because
I had already figured out this had nothing at all to do
with Tavious.
"You know what? This is bullshit, Saadia. The writing is on the wall. It's on the wall because your reaction
to the major on the recorder shows who you really have
feelings for. So stop the crap. I have a friend who has
already spent over half his life in prison and more than
likely will go back if you continue this game."
Saadia didn't respond.
I had said all I wanted to say to her. I started to walk
back down the hallway to let Rossi know that we were
going to have to knock the door down in order for her
to talk to us. Just as I got halfway down the hall, I could
hear the door unlock and Saadia appears.

I looked back at her but my instincts directed me to keep walking and guide her away from her room, then sit down in the living room in a chair across from Rossi. When Rossi saw Saadia he turned the camcorder off and set it next to him on the couch. Soon she was standing before us, deflated.

"Okay, what do you want to know?"

Chapter 66

Who would have thought that Saadia and the major had been lovers going on three years ever since they met at the Quiver Club? It turns out that Saadia was doing an undercover story about the underground sex alternate lifestyle in Atlanta. The major was investigating gambling allegations among other illegal ties within the organization when they met, which damn sure got Rossi's attention. Once Saadia starting talking we couldn't get her to stop, which was good, but we had a deadline to help Tavious from surrendering to police.

"So, tell us about these murders and how they're connected?" I asked her.

"Which one?" She was so blunt. Cold.

"All of them," Rossi pressed.

"Well, we knew Amara," she admitted. She could tell she had our full attention. "Let's put it like this. She starting talking."

"Talking?" Rossi repeated.

"Yes, talking about Tavious and how much fun they were going to have once he got out of prison."

"She knew you guys that well?"

"Yes, Amara was quite well known. She didn't hang out with a lot of people. We all met at the same time. From there we became play partners," she explained.

"So, what happened? How'd she die?" I asked.

"She started talking about what they had planned. The major told me one night that there was no way someone who has been in jail for twenty years would come out and live a life like that without having something stashed."

Rossi and I looked at each other.

"Something like what?" Rossi wanted to know.

"Money," she said point blank.

"So, the major asked to see her," she said. "You know, like a play night. When Amara agrees the major killed her—she never told me how, but she didn't find the money so she had her unit go into the house with one of Ely's dogs to find it."

"That's how Ely was connected?" Rossi wanted to know.

"Right," Saadia confirmed.

"But why kill 'im?"

"He knew too much and Tavious told me that Ely was holding him at bay for the missing money, that Ely knew the major's unit had just pulled out the house with his dogs."

"So, Ely was never owed the money by Tavious," I made sure.

"No, he was killed because he knew too much. He heard too much chatter during the raid and let what little information he did find out get him killed."

"But Tavious told me he talked to one dealer who sold the note."

Saadia kind of chuckled. "Ely promised him a cut. He admitted to it before he was killed."

"By who, though?" I asked her.

"The major never told me. She did say it was someone who fought her tooth and nail on it though."

"You mean they didn't want to do it?"

"So much that they threatened to blow the whistle on everything she was doing," she said.

I automatically thought about Rossi's snitch, Ganes, who could be the one. But he was in the wind now and that wasn't our main concern. As far as I was concerned Ely's murder was on the major since she was the ring leader, and we had to let that be known.

Chapter 67

Finally Saadia gave in and let us know that when we pulled up behind her she was on her way to meet with the major. They had planned to get away and regroup in Miami to think about what they were going to do concerning starting their lives together. She didn't give too much information but she babbled about how Atlanta had become somewhat acceptable to gay couples, but their announcement and walk in the lifestyle as being out would put way too much recognition on them to enjoy themselves as a couple. Their flight was for seven in the evening and the major was expecting her at five.

"So, you know there's no way we can let you run off into the sunset with your girlfriend with Tavious taking the fall," I let her know.

Saadia thought for a second with a blank stare on her face. "I don't care anymore. How did I fall for her *all us* bullshit anyway? I feel like such a fool. She can take her girlfriend and cash, and burn in hell for all I care."

Rossi acknowledged, "But it's not like she knows that you know about this tape. She'll be waiting for you," he said.

"So what?" she snapped.

"So, you have to help us," I told her. "Make her admit to the murders."

"Hell, show us the money, too," Rossi suggested.

Saadia gave the major up without a second thought. She called her to say that she was on the way over so they could leave as planned to Miami. I rode with Saadia as Rossi followed closely behind. The trip to the major's was about fifteen minutes. I got on the phone and called Tavious. I relayed that we had not given up and were close to finding out for sure who killed Amara and Ely. I made sure he understood not to turn himself in. Mrs. Bullock passed the message along through Tavious that whatever I had going on had to get done as soon as possible, because she had made a promise that she was going to keep.

When we pulled up to the gated community I quickly understood why the major didn't stay at her home of record. Her salary and whatever else she had going on was most definitely taking care of her expenses, as her community was full of exclusive town homes, with all-brick sides, manicured lawns, and the same German-built bullshit that Rossi enjoyed to drive sparkling for all to see in the driveways.

We get to the major's home and Saadia parked the car and exhaled. I crossed my fingers, hoping that she wasn't having second thoughts about doing her girl. Rossi parked right beside us and looked into our car with wondering eyes. Finally, without a word Saadia took her keys from the ignition, grabbed her purse, and told us to follow her.

There was a black sedan in the driveway with a man inside talking on the phone who barely paid us any attention as we walked past. But when he saw the cars parked behind him he yelled that he was getting ready to leave and we had to move our cars. Saadia told us that he was the driver who had been dispatched to take them to the airport because the major hated parking there. As we approached the door Rossi let Saadia know that we were going inside with her.

Saadia didn't hesitate to knock on the door, and just as if she was waiting with excitement we hear a female with a screeching voice who shouts out, "Baby," and then the door swings open.

Saadia walked in. When the door almost shut Rossi reached in to stop it from closing and we walked in behind her. The major was surprised and gasps when she sees us.

"What . . . Who the hell is this?"

"We're her friends," Rossi told her.

I finally have the chance to get a face-to-face look at the woman who had inflicted so much havoc on so many lives. Major was easy on the eyes, not just on camera. Light skin, five six, no more than 125 with curves and dimples. But there was no denying her nastiness and control she felt she had in every situation, which actually made her ugly at first sight.

She looked directly at Saadia, hard and scolding. "Who are these men?"

"Doesn't matter who we are," Rossi told her, and shut the door behind us. There were only a few seconds that passed before Saadia gave Rossi a nod, directing him in the direction to the room down the hall on the right where she told us the money was in a briefcase in the attic.

He walked to the room and we all could hear the wooden ladder collapse from above the ceiling and his body walking up the ladder to the attic to retrieve the briefcase.

The major didn't need an e-mail to know what Rossi was going for and she moved toward the room, but I grabbed her by the arm and told her he didn't need any help.

"What—are you robbing me? Saadia, you brought these hoodlums into my home to rob me?" she asked.

"They're not hoodlums, you cheating bitch," Saadia mentions.

Major let out a gasp, as I am sure this was not the kind of love she was expecting coming from Saadia's mouth. "What are you talking about?"

"I'm talking about you and how much you like to record your trysts," Saadia told her.

"Trysts? Saadia, what is your problem?"

"My problem? The question is what the hell is your problem?"

"I have no idea what you're talking about."

Saadia held out her hand and I gave her the recording. She turned it on and within a few seconds the major understood exactly what Saadia meant.

Saadia didn't have to say any more. Kiesha Champaign Majors got it and kind of smiled; then, just like I knew she would, she went for the desk drawer in the hallway that Saadia told us she liked to keep her piece in for times like these. I was already two steps in front of her and had my eye on the desk the entire time. I went to the drawer, grabbed the piece, and told Saadia thanks.

"You bitch!" the major shouted. "What else have you told them?"

"She's told us everything. Amara, Ely, it just doesn't stop with you," I let her know.

We heard Rossi come down from the ladder. He was holding two silver briefcases. "Got it," he said.

The major's eyes were fiery red and there wasn't a thing she could do about it. "After all I've done for you," she said to Saadia.

"You did nothing for me, other than convince me to sleep with an ex-con who turned out to be a pretty decent man."

"Well you seemed to enjoy it, you confused heffa."

"I enjoyed the honesty, bitch. He has compassion; you don't. And at least I'm not confused on the fact that you have done nothing since we met but run my feelings into the ground without a care in the world," Saadia confessed. "You got involved behind my back with someone else without any type of conversation or discussion just because you think you're untouchable. My God, you kill people!"

Rossi nodded his head at the ladies while they go at it and walked right past us and out the door.

"So, you guys think you are going to just, what, arrest me and walk out of here with that money?"

I looked at Saadia and she stood looking at me. I said to her, "What money? I don't see any money. Do you?"

Saadia folded her arms. "She spent it all. Probably put it into one of her dirty accounts overseas or something. I will testify to those accounts along with the murders she told me all about, and not just Amara and Ely."

The major lunged at Saadia and I stepped in between and held her away. We heard Rossi blowing the horn outside.

"Well, Major, I'm sure I will be seeing you soon on the news," I let her know.

"Go to hell," she said.

Saadia gives her one last look and all the major can do is watch us walk away without another word.

I call Mrs. Bullock as I ride with Saadia. I promised her I would take her to see Tavious. Mrs. Bullock picks up without delay. I hated to hear the stress in her voice.

"West, is everything okay?"

"Yes, ma'am, it is. It surely is."

Chapter 68

Down south a perfect day usually has something to do with barbeque ribs and all the fixings while being surrounded by those you know and love. And that's exactly what kind of day it was. Mrs. Bullock put her foot into the planning of her annual estate barbeque. There were at least 700 guests all enjoying the food, music, and games that were laid out all over the grounds. It had been months since Tavious was free and clear of going back to prison and of course the money that we lined our pockets with was more than sufficient. But more importantly Kiesha Champaign Majors and her ruthless crime unit had been stopped from continuing with business as usual and turning anyone else who might cross their path into a corpse. The major was on her way to spending more than a few nights next to the very people she put behind bars and it served her right. Turned out the FBI was also investigating all of her alleged criminal activity and the information Saadia was able to supply the bureau implication-free only guaranteed a conviction.

When we all sat down and split the money as promised, I felt it was time for us all to have a heartfelt conversation about being good stewards of our money and trying to touch it only for emergencies. No gambling, no drugs, or long vacations that would quickly become forgotten. Cash was king and who knew if we would ever get another big payday again?

Rossi let us all know that Rita had been pushing him in the same direction with regard to his money; and he let me know that as soon as he walked in the door she was standing with her hand out to put his share in a safe place, because there was no way she was letting him go out and gamble it away.

It didn't surprise me but Tavious and Saadia were trying to patch things up. They were going to try to work out their brief past for a future together. Tavious promised me he would take it slow with Saadia, and I'll be damned if he didn't register for an online Six Sigma class that would teach him everything he needed to know about the lean process to make the shop run more smoothly. But, even more impressive, he and Joyce and Saadia were spending time with Mrs. Bullock, learning about their family past and getting good advice for the future while they made up for lost time.

It took a few days to get back into total good graces with Lauren after I sort of cut her out of our intimacy time, going hard for the money. But the $20,000 I placed in her bank account was good for starters in letting her know that I appreciated her and everything she did for me. When Lauren got the money in her hand she wanted me to know that she had been thinking about mentoring young girls for the longest and the money would be a good source to help her get started.

Mrs. Bullock was all smiles as her shindig was winding down. It was amazing that everyone was there to help her celebrate. Joyce, Tavious, and Saadia were all standing next to her as Lauren sat with me in my car right before we left to go home.

"Thank y'all for coming," Mrs. Bullock said.

Everyone thanked Mrs. Bullock for the invitation.

"I had a really good time," Rita told her as she stood next to their car. "Promise you'll invite me back next year."

"Same here," Rossi suggested.

"I will, if God is able, sweeties," she tells them. "You know every day I wake up I'm surprised to see it, so we'll see and keep praying that I will even be here tomorrow." She smiled.

"Ohh, Momma, you're gonna have many more of these, don't worry," Joyce let her know then kissed her on the cheek.

"That's right, plenty of them," I let her know, and Lauren cosigned my thoughts.

Then I turn the focus on Tavious. "So, Tavious, you know you owe me a car wash right?"

Tavious waved me off then put his arm around Saadia. "Man, that car doesn't need washing. You keep it spotless."

"Don't matter, you promised," I told him; then Saadia mentioned to him that she remembered Tavious telling her so.

"Yeah, yeah, I did. Okay, so what time you want me to pick it up?"

"Whenever you think you're ready to have it." I noticed Mrs. Bullock put her hand over her mouth.

"Man, say what?"

"You heard me. Whenever you're ready to come get your grandfather's car, come get it. This car was meant to be in your family, so when you're ready to take the best care of it possible, it's all yours. Plus, I'm tired of seeing your eyes tearing up every time you see it," I teased.

Giving is a beautiful thing.

ORDER FORM
URBAN BOOKS, LLC
97 N18th Street
Wyandanch, NY 11798

Name: (please print):_____

Address: _____

City/State: _____

Zip: _____

QTY	TITLES	PRICE
	16 On The Block	$14.95
	A Girl From Flint	$14.95
	A Pimp's Life	$14.95
	Baltimore Chronicles	$14.95
	Baltimore Chronicles 2	$14.95
	Betrayal	$14.95
	Black Diamond	$14.95
	Black Diamond 2	$14.95
	Black Friday	$14.95
	Both Sides Of The Fence	$14.95
	Both Sides Of The Fence 2	$14.95
	California Connection	$14.95

Shipping and handling-add $3.50 for 1st book, then $1.75 for each additional book.

Please send a check payable to:
   Urban Books, LLC
Please allow 4-6 weeks for delivery

ORDER FORM
URBAN BOOKS, LLC
97 N18th Street
Wyandanch, NY 11798

Name: (please print): _____

Address: _____

City/State: _____

Zip: _____

QTY	TITLES	PRICE
	California Connection 2	$14.95
	Cheesecake And Teardrops	$14.95
	Congratulations	$14.95
	Crazy In Love	$14.95
	Cyber Case	$14.95
	Denim Diaries	$14.95
	Diary Of A Mad First Lady	$14.95
	Diary Of A Stalker	$14.95
	Diary Of A Street Diva	$14.95
	Diary Of A Young Girl	$14.95
	Dirty Money	$14.95
	Dirty To The Grave	$14.95

Shipping and handling-add $3.50 for 1st book, then $1.75 for each additional book.

Please send a check payable to:

Urban Books, LLC

Please allow 4-6 weeks for delivery

ORDER FORM
URBAN BOOKS, LLC
97 N18th Street
Wyandanch, NY 11798

Name: (please print): _____

Address: _____

City/State: _____

Zip: _____

QTY	TITLES	PRICE
	Gunz And Roses	$14.95
	Happily Ever Now	$14.95
	Hell Has No Fury	$14.95
	Hush	$14.95
	If It Isn't love	$14.95
	Kiss Kiss Bang Bang	$14.95
	Last Breath	$14.95
	Little Black Girl Lost	$14.95
	Little Black Girl Lost 2	$14.95
	Little Black Girl Lost 3	$14.95
	Little Black Girl Lost 4	$14.95
	Little Black Girl Lost 5	$14.95

Shipping and handling-add $3.50 for 1st book, then $1.75 for each additional book.
Please send a check payable to:
    Urban Books, LLC
Please allow 4-6 weeks for delivery

ORDER FORM
URBAN BOOKS, LLC
97 N18th Street
Wyandanch, NY 11798

Name: (please print):_____

Address: _____

City/State: _____

Zip: _____

QTY	TITLES	PRICE
	Loving Dasia	$14.95
	Material Girl	$14.95
	Moth To A Flame	$14.95
	Mr. High Maintenance	$14.95
	My Little Secret	$14.95
	Naughty	$14.95
	Naughty 2	$14.95
	Naughty 3	$14.95
	Queen Bee	$14.95
	Say It Ain't So	$14.95
	Snapped	$14.95
	Snow White	$14.95

Shipping and handling-add $3.50 for 1ˢᵗ book, then $1.75 for each additional book.
Please send a check payable to:
Urban Books, LLC
Please allow 4-6 weeks for delivery

ORDER FORM
URBAN BOOKS, LLC
97 N18th Street
Wyandanch, NY 11798

Name: (please print): _____

Address: _____

City/State: _____

Zip: _____

QTY	TITLES	PRICE
	Spoil Rotten	$14.95
	Supreme Clientele	$14.95
	The Cartel	$14.95
	The Cartel 2	$14.95
	The Cartel 3	$14.95
	The Dopefiend	$14.95
	The Dopeman Wife	$14.95
	The Prada Plan	$14.95
	The Prada Plan 2	$14.95
	Where There Is Smoke	$14.95
	Where There Is Smoke 2	$14.95

Shipping and handling-add $3.50 for 1st book, then $1.75 for each additional book.

Please send a check payable to:
Urban Books, LLC
Please allow 4-6 weeks for delivery